CLAIRE LOWELL—widowed for a second time, she now falls prey to a social-climbing, much younger man.

LISA MILLER HUGHES—her social position improved, she returns to Oakdale a glamorous divorcée, but quickly becomes entangled in a dangerous affair.

TOM HUGHES—he left his unhappy home to face the horrors of Vietnam, and now he's back, involved in an even worse nightmare.

MICHAEL SHEA—caught between the love of two wealthy women, even his considerable charm is not enough to resolve the situation.

Story Editor **Mary Ann Cooper** is America's foremost soap opera expert. She writes the nationally syndicated column *Speaking of Soaps*, is a major contributor to leading soap opera magazines, and has appeared as a guest on numerous radio and television talk shows.

Johanna Boyd, who wrote *Lovers Who Dare*, lives in Larchmont, New York. Besides being a novelist, she writes poetry and plays the piano.

Dear Friend,

Chris and Nancy Hughes have been the glue that has held the Hughes family together since AS THE WORLD TURNS premiered in 1956. But the couple is much more than that to fans of the serial. Over the years, they have represented the best in American family life. Surely there are countless parents who have modeled themselves after the images Chris and Nancy convey.

Book 3, *Lovers Who Dare*, chronicles a severe test of the stability of the Hughes family when son Bob Hughes rebels against his parents and insists on going his own way. Some lessons of life can only be learned with the breaking of a heart, and perhaps this is the lesson in which Bob will become the student.

In books to come, Nancy and Chris Hughes will weather many more family storms. That is why they have endured to this day as the ideal matriarch and patriarch of soap opera.

For Soaps & Serials Books,

Mary Ann Cooper

Mary Ann Cooper

P.S. If you missed Books 1 and 2 of this series see the order form on page 192 which also tells you how to order books in our other Soaps & Serials™ paperback series.

AS THE WORLD TURNS

Lovers Who Dare

PIONEER COMMUNICATIONS NETWORK, INC.

Lovers Who Dare

AS THE WORLD TURNS paperback novels are published and distributed by Pioneer Communications Network, Inc.

SOAPS & SERIALS™ is a trademark of Pioneer Communications Network, Inc.

ISBN: 0-916217-43-4

Printed in the United States of America

10 9 8 7 6 5 4 3 2 1

Chapter One
Off With The Old

Bob Hughes turned into his parents' driveway, shut off the motor, and sat staring into space. At this moment he wasn't feeling too proud of himself. Here he was, a man in his twenties, and with a promising career in medicine, still living with his mother and father. He'd failed as a husband, he'd had a wife but couldn't keep her, and now he was failing as a father. He glanced at his watch. Six-ten! And he was expected at the Stewarts' at seven. Now he could add bad manners to his list.

As he entered the house by the side entrance, he could hear his mother's soft murmur and his son's childish treble.

"But, Grandmother, I ate so many peas."

"And I was hoping you could eat just a few more, sweetie."

Bob stopped in the kitchen doorway. Tom was sitting on a bar stool at the counter, clasping a spoon in one hand and holding a baseball cap on his head with the other. "Look, Daddy! Guess what! She sent me this suit."

Nancy mouthed, "And it's too small for him." She held onto Tom as he climbed down from the stool and smiled as he ran to Bob to be picked up.

Bob studied his son in mock amazement. "Why, it's a Cubs uniform. Tell me, how long have you been with the Chicago Cubs?"

"Since today. She sent me this uniform today, and I wear it all the time." Tom stared into his father's eyes. Then his smile faded and his lower lip began to tremble. "But, Daddy, when's she coming back to me? I want her!"

Bob held his son closer, stroking the silky auburn hair so like Lisa's. "I don't know, son. Maybe . . . I don't know." He looked at his mother for help.

Nancy bustled to the refrigerator and opened the door. "I believe it's time for our dessert, Tommy dear."

"You eat it, Grandma. I'm not hungry anymore." Tom pulled away from Bob and jumped down.

Nancy grabbed at Tom as he passed by her. "But I made Jell-O. Don't you want some nice cherry Jell-O?"

Tom ran down the hall and started up the stairs. "I don't want it!" he yelled. "I hate Jell-O and I hate you! I hate you!" The sound of his voice was muffled as a door slammed somewhere on the second floor.

After a heavy silence Bob said, "Mom, I'm sorry. You know he doesn't hate you. He loves you. You're the most important woman in his life."

Nancy nodded. "I know that. And I know he loves me. But I don't know what to do. It's just that he misses Lisa so very much."

"There's not much I can do about that. I keep hoping he'll forget her," Bob said.

"I'm afraid that's not going to happen." Nancy looked thoughtful. "If only she would stop writing and calling. Sending gifts. Tom gets so upset every time he hears from her."

"She'll stay in touch," Bob said grimly. "Lisa's too vain to let go. She doesn't want to be his mother, but she won't let him forget her. You said the baseball suit was too small?"

"Yes. It's just ridiculous. She sent size three for a large-for-his-age four-year-old. I've been buying sixes for Tommy for ages."

Bob grunted. "That's Lisa. Vague on important details. It's obvious that she doesn't think about him much. Doesn't realize that he's growing and changing, and . . . and unhappy." His voice faltered.

Nancy was hesitant. "Bob, I've been thinking. Maybe if you married again."

Bob laughed. "Trying to get rid of us, Mom?"

Nancy looked horrified.

"Not that I'd blame you. After all, you've raised your family. Now you're stuck with mine."

Nancy broke in. "That's not it at all, darling, and you know it. Surely you realize how much it means to your father and me, having you and the baby with us . . ."

Bob wanted to say, Tom's not a baby, but checked himself as Nancy continued. "I just thought that if you had a home of your own again, maybe Tom would feel more settled. I can't bear to see him so unhappy."

"Neither can I, Mom. But marriage is out," he said flatly. "I don't know anyone I want to marry . . . or anyone who'd have me. Maybe if I spend more time with him . . ." He looked at the wall clock. "Damn it, I'm late. I'm supposed to be at Ellen and David's in twenty minutes. I'll shower, don't have time to shave." He bounded up the stairs, two steps at a time, and into his room.

Ten minutes later he was standing before the mirror,

knotting his tie, when he heard a rustling behind him. Tom was crawling out from under the bed. "Tom, what were you doing there?"

"Hiding."

With a pang Bob remembered that he hadn't even looked for him. "Why were you hiding under my bed?"

"I don't know." Tom climbed onto the bed and crawled under the coverlet.

Bob studied his son's reflection in the mirror. "Hey, fella, isn't this your bedtime?"

"Nope."

"Why not? It's practically seven o'clock."

"But you haven't read to me yet."

Bob turned around to look at his son. "Tom, I'm really sorry, but I can't read to you tonight. I'm going to the Stewarts'."

Tom stared at him. "Are you coming back?"

Bob chuckled. "Of course."

"When?"

"Later. After you're sound asleep. Come on. Let me take you to your room. Grandmother'll be up soon and help you get ready for bed. I'll bet she'll read to you."

Tom scrambled off the bed and ran down the hall, sobbing, "You don't want a little boy! And she doesn't want me either. I'm not going to love you. And I hate her and I hate you and I hate everybody . . ." He ran into his room and with a force surprising in a four-year-old, slammed shut the door and turned the lock.

Bob was right behind him, yanking at the doorknob. He heard a thud and the tinkle of falling glass. Stepping back, he lunged against the door, forcing it open, and ran inside. Tom had thrown a small, heavy toy horse at a framed print of the *Blue Boy*. Now splinters of glass glittered on the green carpet. "Oh, Tommy, what are we going to do with you?" Bob edged toward his son, who stood straight and defiant, glaring up at him.

"Never mind," Nancy said from the doorway. "I'll take care of this. Darling, come here to Grandmother," she cooed, drawing the little boy toward her.

All at once, Tom was in Nancy's arms, crying softly.

"That's all right, baby," Nancy murmured. "Your daddy loves you, Grandmommy loves you, Granddaddy loves you . . ."

Tom seemed not to hear her. As his wails grew louder, Nancy nodded to Bob, indicating that he should leave.

Bob watched the scene for a moment, then feeling useless and guilty, he went back to his room. Taking his tweed jacket from the closet, he put it on, went downstairs and out the front door, still listening to the muffled sobbing of his little boy.

As he drove toward the Stewarts', he couldn't get Lisa out of his mind. Did she have any concept of what she was doing to Tom? How could she be so selfish? She was vain, silly, immature, self-centered. He groaned. He'd put Lisa out of his life. Now why couldn't he stop thinking about her! The hell with her! But blaming Lisa was a waste of time. To be fair, he wasn't entirely without blame. For one thing, they'd married too young. Everyone had tried to tell him. Mom, Dad, the guys at the Phi Delta House . . . but he wouldn't listen.

He'd never forget the night he met Lisa . . . Lisa Miller. He was in his third year of med school. It was near the end of the term and he was studying for finals. Around 2 A.M., a couple of guys stopped by his room and suggested they go for pizza. So they went to

Harvey's, a place just off-campus. Lisa, who'd just gone to work on the night shift, took their order. She was a cute, skinny, feisty kid with big blue eyes and a mass of wavy reddish hair. One of the guys started ribbing her about her red hair. Bob had said, "That's not red. It's titian."

Lisa scowled and said, "What about it!"

When the guys laughed, Lisa flounced off and refused to wait on their table.

The following day after his exam, Bob stopped by the cafe to apologize.

Lisa cried a little . . . she was so embarrassed. She told Bob that she'd just come down to Champaign from Rockford, Illinois. She was hoping to make enough money waitressing to enroll in the university. Bob could see that she had a good mind, but needed some cultural enrichment. He'd take her around. There was a good art museum on campus. They'd go to some foreign films . . . it would be fun. And it was.

Lisa was so different from the girls he knew. She was eager, funny, interested in everyone and everything. She was particularly interested in him. Thought it was wonderful that he was studying to be a doctor. She knew he'd have a wonderful life . . . helping people . . . making money.

After the semester break, he continued to see Lisa. He learned that she grew up on a little farm ten miles from Rockford. Her father died when she was fifteen and her mother was trying to keep the place going. The better he got to know Lisa, the better he liked her. Then one night they became very well-acquainted.

He'd left the library about 9 P.M. and found Lisa huddled under the steering wheel of his MG. She was crying a little, but trying not to let on that she was. She'd lost her job at the cafe and didn't know what to do. Jobs were hard to find, and she did so want to enroll at the university.

He drove around for a while and they talked. When he suggested taking her back to her rooming house, she didn't object. But when they got to her door, she begged him to come in with her for a while. She didn't want to be alone yet, and it was so late the landlady must be asleep. She'd never know that Bob was there. Maybe if Bob would stay with her just until she fell asleep? As he deliberated, Lisa suddenly grabbed him around the neck and gave him a breathless kiss. For an instant he was stunned. Then he kissed her back. It was the first time he'd touched her and he didn't want to let her go. He followed her upstairs to her room and, although they didn't consummate their relationship, they didn't spend the night sleeping, either.

After that night they were together often. Lisa managed to start classes at the university even though her motivation wasn't the desire for an education but, rather, the desire for a marriage partner with a good financial future. Bob's grades started slipping, and he was called up before the dean. When he told Lisa he had to spend more time on the books, she sulked and teased until he gave in.

When Lisa decided, finally, that Bob was the best prospect she had, she arranged to seduce him one night in the back seat of a Chevy she'd borrowed from another school friend.

Looking back, Bob could see that he was the innocent. Most of what he knew about sex came from textbooks, while Lisa seemed to be steeped in the wisdom of the ages.

Until Bob met Lisa, he'd been top student in his class and likely to intern at the hospital of his choice.

Even though his class standing dropped considerably, he did manage to graduate. When Lisa learned that her plan had worked and that she was pregnant, she was able to convince Bob that they could get married and live with his parents while he interned in Oakdale, his home town.

Lisa and Bob moved into his old room. Bob spent most of his time at the hospital, leaving Lisa with Nancy and Chris. From the outset, Lisa was bored. She never offered to help Nancy with the housework and had no interest in or talent for cooking.

When little Tommy was born, Bob and Lisa moved into an apartment of their own with financial help from Bob's parents. Lisa found herself bored with the daily routines of baby care and housework. Bob noticed that she was changing in many ways.

She began leaving the baby with Nancy while she attended art classes in the afternoon one day a week. Then she went to the opera one night. Bob had to work and was unable to join her. While she was there she met, and quickly became involved with, a wealthy man who didn't have to limit himself to the modest life style of a medical intern. Using her art class as an alibi, she spent more and more time with him hoping that he would marry her once she left her husband.

This time, her plan backfired. Lisa was stunned to learn that her millionaire boyfriend had marriage plans that did *not* include *her*. This time, too, she could not manipulate Bob. He did not want to take her back. Lisa left little Tommy with Bob and moved away . . .

Bob pumped the brakes. He'd almost run a light. Better pay attention to the driving and stay under thirty, at least until the boulevard. He switched on the radio. Some woman was singing "Love Is a Many-

Splendored Thing." Bob wasn't so sure. Maybe. Now and then he thought he should have taken Lisa back when she wanted to try again. But things wouldn't have worked out. Someone was bound to have come along and he and little Tom would have had to go through that rejection again. Lisa had an exceptionally bad effect on Tom. Always the flirt, even when she was playing "the mother," she'd nearly love Tom to death, then dump him. Son or lover . . . what do you do about such a woman? Bob had proved to himself that he could live without her. But Tom wanted his mother. And to think, Lisa didn't know what size clothes Tom wore!

Bob considered Nancy's suggestion that he marry again. She could be right. Perhaps there was a nice, attractive, motherly woman out there who'd be willing to marry him. It would be a good thing for Tom, and God knows, he could use a little happiness himself. After being married, he missed living with a woman. He lacked the energy and time for philandering . . . spending nights in strange beds with ladies of brief acquaintance. No way! Maybe a good marriage *was* possible.

Plenty of people had a good marriage the second time around. As a case in point, there was Claire, Ellen's mother. Claire had had a long-lasting, though rocky marriage with Jim Lowell. Widowed, now she was married to Doug Cassen, chief of surgery at Oakdale Memorial. Doug was an absolute rock. And Claire seemed happy these days. Or maybe content was the better word. What else could you ask for? Bob would settle for a lady rock, a nice, quiet, stable, pretty . . . No, no, forget pretty. Not an imperative. He was glad that Claire and Doug were to be at the Stewarts'. Give him a chance to study them, to find out what they were doing right.

He parked at the curb in front of the Stewarts' home. Every light in the house seemed to be on. The place looked big and cheerful. Tonight should be good: stimulating company, a great meal—take his mind off his problems. He glanced at his watch. Damn. He was twenty minutes late. Better stop dawdling. Slamming the car door behind him, he hurried up the front walk and rang the bell.

Chapter Two
The Lost Princess

Ellen, looking beautiful and serene, opened the door. "Come in, Bob! So good to see you."

"Good to see you. Hey, I'm sorry to be late, but something—"

"Came up!" Ellen giggled. "Don't apologize. Remember, I'm married to a doctor. I never plug in the coffeepot until I see the whites of David's eyes." Taking his arm, she ushered him into the living room.

Claire Cassen was sitting in the big armchair beside the fireplace, watching the flames. She reached for Bob's hand as he bent to give her a peck on the cheek. "Tell Nancy I'll call her this week to have lunch."

"She'll love hearing from you." Bob turned and spied Doug Cassen standing nearby with his back to the fire. "Hardly saw you today, Doug. Hear you were pretty busy."

Doug clasped Bob's hand. "Fairly rigorous day, I'd say. Spent most of it in O.R."

A tall, fair-haired woman rose from the sofa.

Bob was surprised. Ellen hadn't mentioned a fourth

dinner guest. "Oh, hello," he said. "I don't believe we've met."

Ellen was laughing. "Give the hostess a chance, Bob. Sandy McGuire, Bob Hughes."

Bob and Sandy spoke in unison. "How do you do." Sandy laughed self-consciously and sat down.

"Now that the introductions are taken care of, I must rush away to the scullery." Ellen hurried out of the room and in the direction of the kitchen.

David came in with a tray of drinks. "Bob! What'll you have? Scotch?"

"On the rocks."

"Thought so. Be back in a flash." As he left the room, a quavering "Mommeee" came from upstairs.

David called, "Dear, I believe you're being paged."

Sandy jumped to her feet. "Oh, Ellen, please let me go." And she was halfway up the stairs.

Ellen called after her, "Thanks, Sandy." Ellen came back into the living room. "Sandy misses her own little boy so much."

Damn, Bob thought. There's probably a husband. "She's an interesting person," he said. "Wonder why we never met before."

"She's not from Oakdale. You explain, Mother. And please excuse me, I must get back to the kitchen if we're to eat before midnight."

Bob looked at Claire. "What's the story?"

Claire shrugged. "Heavens, I only met her tonight. I know very little about her."

David returned with Bob's drink. "Ellen got to know Sandy when they were in prison, Bob. In fact, Ellen says she owes her sanity, maybe her life even, to Sandy. Ellen's very grateful and very fond of her." David went back to the kitchen.

Doug was watching Claire, who was making no

effort to hide her annoyance.

Bob looked from one to the other. "Well, whoever she is, I'd like to take her home with me. She's good with kids. Have you noticed? Paul or Dan, whichever one it was, has stopped crying."

"One might wonder how she stopped the crying."

Ellen returned in time to overhear Claire's remark. "Mother," she said in a low voice, "please don't be like this. Sandy is dear and good and wonderful and she's had a perfectly awful life. Anything I can do for her I will. I owe her so much."

"I'm sure she's as noble as you say, dear." Claire looked at Bob. "But don't you think it's a bit much, her coming here straight out of prison, expecting to be rehabilitated!"

"Mother! Sandy was paroled three weeks ago. I told you, she's been in Chicago with her little boy. But she wants to make a new life for herself and Jimmy. I urged her to come here because I want to help her. She means a great deal to me."

Claire rolled her eyes. "A bleeding heart. What did I ever do to produce a bleeding heart?"

Doug touched Claire's shoulder. "You imparted your own generosity of spirit and your compassion for the human condition. That's what you did, my dear."

Claire looked up at Doug, her eyes shining. "Oh, you!" she said.

"You still haven't told me anything about Sandy," Bob said.

"What would you like to know?"

There was Sandy, standing not three feet away. Bob wondered how much she'd heard. No point in trying to smooth things over now. Might as well be blunt. "I want to know everything about you, Sandy."

Ellen ran to Sandy and hugged her. "Sandy, please

don't be hurt. No one meant to be unkind."

"I know," Sandy said stiffly. "But you don't owe me a thing. Really! And I don't want to cause problems for you. So I'd better leave." Sandy turned to go back upstairs. "I'll get my things."

Ellen was almost in tears. "Please, Sandy! Please don't go! You know that David and I want you here. Now please come back in here and sit down. Dinner's almost ready." As Sandy paused on the stairs, Ellen rushed on. "If you leave now, I'll never forgive myself. Please, Sandy."

Sandy smiled at her and came back down the stairs. "This is an awkward situation for all of you, I know. And it's particularly awkward for me. Maybe it would be easier if we talked . . . brought everything into the open."

Bob could feel the back of his neck tingling. This lady had guts. She was a lot more than good legs and big brown eyes. But he'd better stop staring and pay attention to what Ellen was saying.

"I guess it would, Sandy. But later. The roast is ready, so let's eat now. Follow me."

When they were in the dining room, Ellen said, "I think I'll keep the newlyweds together. So, Mother, you sit on David's right, Bob, you sit next to me, and Sandy beside David."

Bob smiled at Sandy and said, "A splendid arrangement." He held the chair for her, then seated himself.

Sandy sat quietly, her mouth set in a fixed smile, as the conversation flowed around her. Claire thought last year's Pulitzer winner, *The Old Man and the Sea*, was "bloody boring," and that went for Hemingway generally. Even though Bob hadn't read the thing, he tried to ask Sandy if she had. But she was oblivious. He could tell she wasn't listening to the others either. What world was she in? He wished he could draw her into his. Finally he said, rather too loudly, he thought, "How do you like Oakdale?"

Sandy seemed startled. "I beg your pardon? Oh, oh, very much. Of course I haven't seen all of it."

"Some parts are better than others." Why did he say that? She probably thought he was some doddering old geezer, getting ready to pinch her. But he'd better not falter now. Ask her another question. "When did you get in town?"

"Just this afternoon. I felt terrible when I discovered that Ellen and David were having guests to dinner."

"Ellen didn't mind. She just set another place. And I'm glad you're here. Now I'm not an extra man."

She smiled politely. "I'm pleased to save you from that fate. Have you known Ellen long?"

"All her life. Ellen and my sister Penny were always 'best friends' when they were growing up. They're still close."

Sandy's eyes widened. "Of course! You're Penny's brother, the doctor. Ellen has told me so much about her. I'm pleased to meet you!"

They shook hands.

Claire nudged Doug, but he ignored her and continued talking to David.

Bob was studying her face. She noticed and began to fidget. "I'm sorry. I don't mean to stare at you, but you really are beautiful."

"Please," Sandy said, "you embarrass me."

"Sorry. I was wondering, how long do you plan to be here?"

"I don't know. I want to stay away from Chicago—that's the best thing for me, I think. Actually, I'd like to find a job here in Oakdale."

"You would!" Bob sounded a little too eager, even to

himself. "Maybe I can help."

"Please don't trouble yourself," Sandy said stiffly. "I can manage."

"Of course you can. But in the meantime, how about taking that chip off your shoulder?"

"Another bleeding heart?" Sandy's tone was caustic.

"If you like. Now tell me about your son. Jimmy? Is that his name?"

All at once Sandy's hostility was gone. "Yes. Jimmy's seven. I've missed him so much. You can't imagine." Her words came out in a rush. "My mother took care of him—he's still with her—while I was away. I was in there for two years and now . . ." Her voice faltered. "It's as if he doesn't remember me."

"Surely things will change once you're together." Bob tried to sound convincing.

"That's what I think." Her eyes were misty. "I can hardly wait until he's all mine again."

"What about your husband?"

"We're divorced."

Bob tried not to look pleased. "So am I."

"How sad for you. I'm sorry. How long have you been divorced?"

"Two years. How long have you been free?" Bob flushed. "That's not what I meant!"

Sandy grinned. "I know what you meant. Roy and I have been divorced for three weeks. The decree became final soon after I left the facility."

"Facility?"

"That's what the state calls it, a minimum security facility. I like that word better than prison . . . jail . . . or . . ."

"Slammer?" Bob said helpfully.

Sandy began to giggle. When everyone stopped talking, she said, "He's very funny. He really is."

Bob looked pleased.

Claire was annoyed. "Please share the *bon mot* with us. We're so dull on this side of the table."

Doug patted Claire's hand. "Now, dear, we can't ask these youngsters to repeat an entire conversation."

"Youngsters!" Ellen hooted. "I love that. Don't you, Sandy!"

Sandy didn't answer.

Damn Claire! Sometimes Bob enjoyed her sarcasm. But not tonight! She shouldn't be picking on this defenseless, fragile woman. But for some reason, Claire was out for blood. A diversion was in order. He raised his wine glass. "A toast to our hostess. Ellen, you've outdone yourself. This dinner is even more than I expected it to be."

"Hear! Hear!" David said.

"Everything is lovely, dear," Claire said. She turned to Bob. "Praise from you is high indeed. You must be a gourmet because Nancy Hughes is a marvelous cook."

"Thank you," Bob said. "I'll tell her." He turned to Sandy. "Claire's referring to my mother. For the present my son and I live with my parents."

"I see," Sandy said.

Bob was afraid she saw more than he wished. "Mother's awfully good with my little boy," he said lamely. "There's been so much disruption in his life. Anyway, I try to keep him as happy as possible."

"How old is your son?"

"He's four. And he's very sensitive and aware."

"I know. It's amazing how sharp children are these days. I was stunned when I saw Jimmy. How he's changed in two years! I can't get over it." She shook her head. "I don't even know him."

How awful everything was for this woman. Bob wanted to say something that would sound positive.

"But that's going to change when you get a home of your own and can be with him all the time."

"I know," she said.

"And if you won't bite my head off I'd like to repeat, maybe I can help you find a job." When she didn't answer, he continued. "What kind of work do you do? Secretarial? Are you a teacher?"

"I worked in the prison library. Both Ellen and I worked there."

"That's great. Then you can be a librarian!"

"No, I can't. I never went to college. And I don't know why I was put in the prison library, but I was glad to be there!"

"I can imagine."

"Poor Ellen was put in the laundry at first. It was terrible."

"It was." Ellen said. "Beyond words. But thank heaven I met Sandy and she was able to pull a few strings."

"How did you do that?" Bob asked.

"I really don't know," she said quickly.

"Lucky thing you met a lady with clout, Ellen," Bob said.

Sandy tensed. "You don't take anything seriously, do you?"

"Oh, but I do," Bob said earnestly. "But when terrible things happen that can't be explained, I guess I can't deal with them." When Sandy didn't answer, he floundered on. "I know . . . everyone knows that Ellen should never have been in prison. And I know you. You should never have been there either."

"What a ridiculous thing to say. You don't know me."

"But it's true. I can't explain it, but I know you."

Sandy stared into her wine glass. "Wish I did."

Bob smiled. "I'll tell you at dinner tomorrow night."

"Thank you, but I can't," Sandy said.

"Then how about the night after that?"

Sandy laughed uneasily. "Thanks, but I really couldn't." She turned to David. "I love your house. It's very beautiful."

"I agree, Sandy," David answered. "But it isn't my house. I'm here through the good graces of my wife."

"And you'd better watch your step, or out you go," Ellen said with mock severity.

"Ellen's great-grandfather Lowell built this house," Claire said.

At last Sandy has said the right thing, Bob thought. *She's introduced one of Claire's favorite subjects. Hope she doesn't dwell on it too long.*

"Ellen has lived here all her life." Claire's glance traveled around the huge room with its walnut paneled walls. "For a long time I lived here too. And now I don't."

"Because now you live with me in my bachelor's digs." Doug smiled at her.

Claire looked into Doug's eyes. "And I like them best of all."

"They seem very happy," Sandy said to Bob.

"Which means there's hope for us." Bob was pleased to note that Sandy seemed flustered.

"Tell me more about this wonderful house, and Ellen's great-grandfather," Sandy said.

"I never met him, of course. But according to my grandfather, the old Mr. Lowell came here around 1850 and bought two thousand acres of swampland. Even though he paid fifteen cents an acre, the old-timers thought he was crazy. Then he laid tiles, drained the land, and wound up with two thousand acres of top soil two feet deep."

Sandy laughed. "I don't know enough even to follow

this story. But I suppose he made money."

"That he did. He got rich enough to build this big yellow brick house and fill it with fine furniture. His son, who was Ellen's grandfather, grew up to be Judge Lowell and the senior partner in his own law firm. Later on he hired my father as his clerk . . . and here I am!"

Sandy was smiling. "I love stories with happy endings."

"So do I! Now about dinner . . ."

"Please, Bob. Right now I'm not very good company. Maybe . . ."

"I'll try again."

"That could be a mistake. Has anyone told you why I was in prison?"

Bob shook his head. "No. But I'd like you to tell me about it."

Sandy took a deep breath. "Okay, my husband Roy, my son Jimmy and I lived in Chicago. Roy was a bank teller in the Loop area and I was a clerk at a cosmetics counter in Marshall Field's."

Bob wondered if Sandy was aware that everyone was listening. Then he saw her glance at Claire, who seemed spellbound. Sandy continued.

"We didn't make much money, but we were getting along. Then one day we met in the parking lot, as usual, and started home. Roy asked me to drive because he wanted to stop at a liquor store that was on our way. They were having a sale on wine." She paused. "You know, this all sounds so crazy. And nobody believes the truth. The judge certainly didn't." She glanced at Ellen. "*She* believes me."

Bob waited for her to continue, hoping Sandy wouldn't notice the skeptical look on Claire's face.

"There was a parking space near the store. Roy got out of the car but before he got to the door, there were shots and a man ran out of the store. He threw a package at Roy and disappeared into the crowd. Suddenly Roy was back in the car, yelling, 'Let's get out of here.' And we did. I drove as fast as I could but the bullets were still coming at us. One hit a rear tire and the car stopped moving. Police took us to the station. It was terrible. Roy and I didn't know that man. We'd never seen him before in our lives." Sandy sat for a moment, looking around the table. Then she glanced at her watch and stood. "Will you please excuse me?" She looked at Ellen. "I'm going to call Mother . . . and maybe speak to Jimmy." She strode out of the room.

No one spoke for a minute, then Claire exploded. "Well, drat! She never finished her story."

"What more do you want, Mother?"

"The rest of the story, of course. And I have questions. What did the stranger throw at Roy?"

"I can fill you in, Mother. All this is still too painful for Sandy to talk about. The stranger threw a shopping bag filled with the contents of the store's cash register. Ergo, Sandy was an accomplice, unwitting or not."

Claire looked at her companions. "A show of hands. How many buy Sandy's story?"

"I do," Ellen said.

"My dear, I must have omitted something in our mother-daughter sessions. This is the most highly unlikely yarn I've ever heard."

"I believe every word," Bob said.

Doug nodded. "So do I. However, I'm not entirely convinced the stranger was unknown to Roy. I'd like to know more about that husband of Sandy's."

"I'm curious about him too," David said. "Although Sandy may believe in his innocence, she agreed to divorce him when he asked her to."

Bob looked thoughtful. "Wonder why he wanted the

divorce. Was it for her sake or his own?"

"He's noble, I suppose," David answered. "He was sentenced for ten years. Maybe he wanted some options for Sandy. Also there's the child to think of . . ." His voice trailed off as he saw Ellen's wistful expression. "I remember other conversations along those lines."

Ellen forced a smile. "Who'll have coffee?"

"Not I," Claire said. "I wouldn't sleep a wink." She looked at Doug. "And you'd better not drink any either."

Doug shrugged.

Claire glared across the table at Bob. "And you! I don't like your attitude."

"What do you mean, Claire."

"It's obvious. You're attracted to this woman."

"Mother!" Ellen nearly dropped the cup she was filling with coffee. "That's none of your business."

"Yes, it is my business! Nancy Hughes is my best friend. Chris too! When she learns that Bob met a former convict at my daughter's house . . ."

Ellen gritted her teeth. "Mother, must I remind you that your daughter is also an ex-con?"

"Don't talk that way. Everything was different in your case. You were innocent!"

"And so is Sandy." Ellen looked Claire in the eye.

"Ladies, please let's change the subject," David said.

"I agree." Doug got to his feet. "Well, dear," he said to Claire. "Pity to eat and run, but I have a long day ahead of me tomorrow. Lovely dinner, Ellen." He put his hand on the back of Claire's chair.

"Just a minute. I haven't had my say," Claire snapped.

"Of course you haven't. Nevertheless. Shall we?" He waited.

Claire watched Bob rise from the table. "Will you be leaving now?"

"I don't think so, Claire. Guess I'll hang around for a bit. Maybe I'll get the chance to say good night to Sandy. I'd hate being rude. Wouldn't you?"

"Wouldn't think of it." Claire got up and stalked out of the dining room, calling over her shoulder, "We're leaving now, Ellen, David. Such a lovely time. Give our love to the little boys."

Ellen hurried after them, but they were already out the door. She sighed and returned to the dining room. David and Bob looked at one another and began to laugh.

"Ellen," David gasped, "your mother is a terrible woman."

Ellen was laughing too. "She's awful." She shook her head in amazement. "But I'm afraid she hurt Sandy. I know Mother doesn't mean to be cruel, she just . . ."

"She doesn't?" David sounded doubtful.

"I agree with you, Ellen," Bob said. "Claire has never intentionally hurt anyone in her life. Sometimes she's a little tactless—"

David hooted. "Tactless! Sometimes I'd like to wring her neck." He made a face at Ellen. "It's not that I don't adore your mother . . ."

"I'll be leaving too," Bob said. "But I really would like to say good night to Sandy."

At that moment Sandy walked through the door. She looked happy. "Sorry to have been away so long, but I was talking to Jimmy."

"Sandy! That's wonderful!" Ellen said.

"And he said he missed me already." She looked at Bob. "And I haven't been gone a day. He missed me!"

"Don't blame him," Bob said.

"Things are going to work out. I know they will. I'll

get a job . . . and I'll find an apartment for us . . ."

Ellen hugged her. "I know you will, Sandy. Good things are going to start happening for you. It's time."

Sandy looked at Ellen and then at David. "You're both so good to me."

She's really a stunner, Bob thought. *And she's tall . . . nearly as tall as I am.* "Wait," he said. "Let me be good to you too. How about having dinner with me the night after the night after tomorrow night?"

"I'd love to. Thank you very much!" She kissed his cheek.

"Well, great," Bob stammered, suddenly confused by a sense of all this having happened before. "Then, uh, until three nights from tonight. An outstanding evening, Ellen, David. Good night."

He hurried out of the room, out the front door, and into his car, wondering what he was doing, trying to involve himself with a mysterious blonde from Chicago.

Chapter Three
A Proposal Of Sorts

The morning following the dinner party, Sandy woke up early, showered, and refused to eat breakfast, despite Ellen's urging. She felt too tense for anything except a cup of coffee. She studied the help wanted columns and a little before nine, set out on her quest for employment. During interviews she tried to avoid mentioning her prison experience but usually failed. Maybe she should fabricate an account of her past two years. But what if someone should check her story? No. It was better to be direct with people.

Everyone who interviewed her was polite, sometimes too polite. And wouldn't you know! They were fresh out of openings. Her adventures the following days were similar. She returned to the big yellow brick house on Lincoln Avenue about four in the afternoon, tired and defeated. What was the use! She'd never get a job—she'd have to go back and live with her mother after all.

Ellen was waiting for her in the living room. Wouldn't she like a cup of tea? "I'd love one, Ellen," she answered. What she really would have liked was a good stiff shot of bourbon. She wondered what Ellen would do if she said that. Swoon, maybe. That's what the gentry did. They swooned and didn't drink anything except good sherry.

Ellen returned to the living room with a delicate china tea set and plate of oatmeal cookies on a tray. "I baked these for the boys this afternoon," she said.

"They're wonderful," Sandy answered. "I wonder if I'll ever have a place to bake cookies for Jimmy."

"Of course you will. You must start believing in the future, Sandy."

"Maybe I should stop believing in the past. I'd like to forget all of it, except Jimmy."

Ellen's blue eyes seemed to darken. "Learn to live with the past, Sandy. That's what I'm trying to do."

"I'll work on it, after I learn to cope with the here and now." Sandy stifled a yawn. "If you'll excuse me, I'll go to my room and rest before dinner."

"That's a good idea," Ellen said. "When is Bob coming by for you?"

"Bob! I'd completely forgotten." Sandy made a wry face. "I wish I hadn't said I'd go."

"It'll do you good. Now run on and take your nap."

As she climbed the stairs to the second floor, Sandy tried to make her mind go blank, but it was hard to forget the condescending smile of the personnel woman she'd waited so long to see at that big store. Her grating manner. Oh, well, she must put that sort of thing out of her mind. She drew the curtains and got into the huge old cherry bed with the ornately carved headboard that had been a favorite of Ellen's great-grandfather. She closed her eyes and thought of Roy.

What is he doing at this minute? she wondered. Is he coming off his shift in the machine shop? She hadn't heard from him in over three months. Her lawyer had advised against writing to Roy or going to see him. Now that the divorce was final, maybe there wasn't a reason to see him or talk to him. The letters they'd exchanged had been monitored. She'd been afraid to write the things she felt. Surely Roy had felt the same way. She guessed that explained why his letters had seemed so cold.

Poor Roy. In her heart Sandy was positive that he'd known nothing about the robbery of the liquor store. And of course he hadn't known what happened to the stolen money. If he'd known he would have told the authorities where it was. Then neither she nor Roy would ever have been in prison!

Dear Roy! She owed him so much, everything that was good in her life, even some of the things that hadn't been so good. How long ago had they met? Ten years? No, it must have been nine. She was twenty-four now. She'd been fifteen at the time they'd met and Roy had been sixteen. She smiled, remembering the first time she'd seen him.

It was the Saturday after Christmas, and Roy's family had moved into the building Sandy and her mother lived in. She'd stared out the window, watching Roy help the movers unload the van. He'd been so slim and so graceful. She'd said to her mother, "That new kid looks like a tango dancer with that shiny black hair. I'll bet his eyes are blue. Maybe he's Spanish."

"Looks black Irish to me," her mother had answered. "And don't you go taking up with him!"

"You needn't worry, Mama," Sandy had said. "I must be a foot taller than he is. He won't pay any attention to me." And it had never occurred to her that he would.

But the first school day in the new year, Roy was

standing on the steps in front of the building when she came out. Hoping he wouldn't notice her, she hunched her shoulders and looked down at the walk as she strode past him. "Hey, Mama Tree Top," he called after her. "You going to the high school?" Sandy nodded her head and kept going. Roy was close behind her. "So wait up. I thought I'd go with you and let you show me the ropes."

Sandy stopped and beamed down at him. "I'd just love to."

That afternoon after school, Sandy looked for Roy, thinking he might want to walk home with her. Angie and Francine, her best friends, were watching her. "What are you doing? Waiting for the new guy?" Francine asked.

"Good heavens, no!" Sandy answered. "I think I mighta dropped my fountain pen around here someplace."

"Forget it!" Angie said. "I saw that new guy leaving fifteen minutes ago. He walked out with Evelyn Calvert."

"So what!" Sandy said, vowing to herself that she'd never speak Roy McGuire again as long as she lived. "I've got to hurry home. Mama wants me to get supper."

"So what else is new? Your mother always wants you to get supper," Angie said.

Sandy could hear them giggling as she ran down the steps and headed up the street. *They're making fun of me again*, she thought. But she didn't dare get mad at them. They were her only friends, even if they did call her "hillbilly" and "redneck." She couldn't help being from Tennessee. Anyway she'd lived in Chicago for two years. Didn't that count for anything?

When Sandy got home, she was surprised to see Roy

waiting at the door to her apartment. Mama wouldn't be home yet. How could she invite him in? "I heard you left with Evelyn Calvert," she said as she fitted the key in the lock.

"Is that her name? I don't have a key to my place yet," Roy said. "I want to wait here until my folks get home." When Sandy didn't answer he said, "Look, you're 318. I'm 418. Directly above you. When I hear my folks walking around upstairs, I'll go home. Okay?"

"Okay," Sandy said and opened the door. She went straight to the kitchen and took two bottles of soda from the refrigerator. "Want one?"

"Never touch 'em," Roy said. "And you shouldn't either. They're bad for your teeth. Do you have any milk?"

Sandy poured a glass for him and they sat at the kitchen table in companionable silence. After a while Sandy said, "What do you think of the school?"

"It's all right," Roy answered. "Any school's good as long as you study. And I do. I want enough money to move out of this end of town and I want to be somebody."

Sandy took a long drink from the pop bottle. "What do you plan to do when you grow up?"

"I'm not sure yet. And I guess I'm as grown up as I'll ever be. Say, how tall are you?"

"Five-eleven." Sandy rose from the table, rinsed out her bottle and placed it on the sink drainboard.

"That's great," Roy said with enthusiasm. "But you ought to stand up straight and throw back your shoulders. That way your chest will stick out, but your stomach won't."

"Gosh! You're mean!" Sandy hoped she wasn't going to cry.

"Don't give me that dirty look," Roy said. "I'd like to help you. And you really should take off some weight." He looked at her with narrowed eyes. "At least twenty pounds, I'd say. How much do you weigh?"

"I'm not going to tell you. Now will you please go? My mother's going to be home soon and she'll be mad at me if she sees you here." Sandy opened the door to the hall and waited.

"Don't be silly. I won't leave until my folks get home. And another thing, you shouldn't wear all that makeup. It makes you look like a sleaze."

"If I'm so awful to look at, just stay away from me. Now get out!" Sandy ran into her room, slamming the door behind her, and fell across her bed. She hated this stuck-up know-it-all. Roy opened the door and smiled at her. "I thought you'd gone. Now get out of here."

Roy sat on the edge of the bed. "Don't be a jerk. I like you or I wouldn't bother. I'm just trying to set you straight. You can be beautiful. Now listen to me. Wash that gunk off your face, throw away those red glass earrings and stop fooling around with your hair."

Sandy stared up at him in amazement. No one, not even her mother, had ever talked to her this way. Roy was stroking her hair. "Look at this," he said. "It's frizz. Now don't curl your hair anymore. Just let it be natural and you'll have real class."

"I'll show you real class!" Sandy's mother was coming toward Roy with her right hand clenched into a fist. "Now beat it!" She glared at Sandy. "I'll deal with you later, missy!"

Roy sauntered out of the room. At the door he turned. "Good afternoon, Mrs. Harper, Sandy." He stepped into the hall and closed the door behind him, leaving Sandy cowering on the bed.

"Now, Mama, this isn't what you're thinking. Roy was talking to me about good grooming."

"Was he now! Tell me the truth, Sandy. Did that boy touch you?"

"Not much. He was just kind of patting my head."

"Are you sure that's all he was doing?"

"Yes, Mama. That's all!" Sandy got up and went into the kitchen. "I was just getting ready to start supper."

"That's a funny way to go about it." Elsie Harper sat at the kitchen table and yanked her hat off. "Now, Alessandra," she began.

Here we go, Sandy thought. How she hated listening to her mother's harangues, her constant rehashings of the past. Most of the time Sandy didn't know what her mother was talking about.

"You know I do the best I can for you," she was saying. "It's mighty hard to bring up a young girl with no help from anyone. If only your daddy hadn't been killed in the war, we could have had a good life down home. We wouldn't have had to come all the way up here just so I could get a job. And some job it is too. Workin' in the packin' plant is giving me terrible rheumatism in my hands. They keep it so cold in there!" She rubbed her hands together. "And they hurt. All the time."

"Mama, I know."

"You don't know at all. You don't know what it does to me, goin' off to work, leavin' you to come home to empty rooms, gettin' into bed with God knows who."

"But, Mama, I didn't get into bed. I just got so mad, I went in there to lie down. I wanted to get away from him!"

"You sure tried gettin' away from that boy! Now listen to me, girl. I want you to behave yourself, do well in school, and be somebody. You don't want to turn out like me!"

Sandy put her arms around her mother. "That wouldn't be so awful. I want to be a good person like you, Mama."

"All right then. Now promise me you won't have anything more to do with that boy."

"I promise, Mama." Anything to get Mama off the subject of Roy. "Guess I'd better start peeling the potatoes."

On the way home from school the next afternoon, Sandy stopped at the little lunchroom on the corner with Angie and Francine to get a pizza. Just as Sandy was taking her first bite, Roy rapped on the window and mouthed, "Pizza's a no-no."

"What's he want?" Francine asked.

"I don't know." Sandy put the food back on her plate. All at once she wasn't hungry anymore.

"I don't know what's got into you, Sandy," Angie said.

"That new guy sure is cute," Francine said. She gave Sandy a hard look. "There's something different about you today. I've got it! No lipstick!"

"I noticed," Angie said. "She looks like she's going to a funeral. And what did you do to your hair?"

"Nothing," Sandy answered.

As the months passed, Sandy could feel herself changing. She was losing weight, seeing less of Angie and Francine, and she was studying. Usually she walked home from school with Roy. Occasionally he came into the apartment with her, but made a point of leaving at least twenty minutes before her mother was due home. They talked a lot about what they planned to do when they were older. Sometimes they did homework together. Sandy thought Roy was wise and wonderful. She wished her mother knew him better. Then she wouldn't mind that Sandy saw a lot of him.

Elsie Harper noted the change in Sandy and was pleased. She did worry about the weight loss. "You feelin' all right, hon? You're lookin' kind of peaked."

"I'm fine, Mama. I guess I'm finally losing my baby fat."

"I hope that's it. But you do put me in mind of your Aunt Lolly, your father's sister. She was tall and skinny. Then she got the consumption and died when she was hardly older than you."

"Mama, people don't even have consumption now. And I feel fine."

"That's what you say." But Mrs. Harper continued to complain.

One Saturday afternoon Sandy told her mother she was going to the movies with Angie and Francine. Instead she met Roy, and they took the bus to a part of the city Sandy had never seen. They strolled along Lake Shore Drive, looking into the windows of elegant shops. Roy stopped before one window, saying, "Now that's it. That's the dress you should wear."

Sandy appraised the dress. "I don't know, Roy. It's a pretty color, but don't you think it's kind of plain?"

"That's the point, Sandy. It's simple and good. And it's the kind of dress you're going to wear every day when I get rich."

Sandy could feel a warmth inside her rib cage spread to her shoulders and down her arms, making her fingers tingle. Never, until this moment, had Roy's plans for the future included her. "I guess that will be all right," she said softly.

"Good! Then that's settled. We're engaged." Roy put his arm around her waist and they walked on in silence.

The following Saturday, Sandy arranged to meet Roy again. But this time she was to walk up the flight of stairs to his parents' apartment. She'd never met Roy's mother and father and was curious about them. Roy was waiting for her and opened the door before she could knock.

Sandy looked around the living room. "Where are your mother and father?"

"They're sorry to miss you, but they had to go out for the rest of the day. They won't be home until late tonight," Roy said. "They want to meet you another time."

"Oh." Sandy sat on the sofa. For the first time she felt uneasy being with Roy.

"How about a glass of orange juice first?"

"Are we going out?"

"Not just yet." Roy sat beside her and pulled her toward him and kissed her until she was out of breath.

When she could shove him away, Sandy stared at him in amazement. "What are you doing? I'm going home!"

Before she could get up, he grabbed her again and pinned her down to the sofa, covering her mouth with his. Sandy squirmed and kicked and finally pushed him away. "Roy, why are you doing this?" She stood and straightened her skirt. "Really, I don't know what's gotten into you."

"I thought you loved me," Roy said. "We're engaged, aren't we?"

"I do love you and, yes, we are engaged. But I don't know why you're being so mean and rough."

"I'm sorry, Sandy." He put out his hand and Sandy took it. "Come with me." He led her into his room, drew Sandy down on the bed beside him. "Don't you want to marry me, Sandy?" he asked softly.

Soon he was beside her, covering her with kisses. Suddenly she tensed—she wanted to be out of the bed, out of the room, and in her own room.

At last she was able to slide away from him. She glanced at Roy, who was sleeping, and slipped out the door and ran all the way down the stairs to her mother's apartment.

Elsie Harper looked up from her paper. "Well, you look a fright. What happened?"

"Nothing much," Sandy answered. "The movie was over early and I didn't feel too well, so I came on home."

"You'd better get to bed early tonight," Elsie said and went back to her paper.

Sandy filled the tub with hot water and took a long bath. She told her mother she wasn't hungry and went to bed. But she lay awake for a long time. Of course she loved Roy, but she liked most of all just to be with him, talk with him. That other business was awful. She wondered if she was going to have a baby.

That spring Roy graduated from high school with honors. He got a job keeping books for a small electrical appliance store. He wanted to go to college, but that was out. His mother had lost her job and a good part of his paycheck was needed at home.

When Roy insisted, Sandy continued to meet him in his parents' apartment when they were out for the evening. She hated the physical part of their relationship but tried not to let Roy see how she felt. He'd think a lot less of her if he knew. Anyway, she must have something wrong with her. Angie and Francine talked about sex a lot and they seemed to like it. Sandy wondered how much they really knew.

Sandy was well into her senior year of high school and making good grades when she realized she was pregnant. She hated to tell Roy, knowing he'd have a fit. And he did. The first thing he said was, "We'll have to have this taken care of." Sandy was glad that he said "we." Then Roy told her he knew a guy at work who'd be sure to know where Sandy could go.

But the more Sandy thought about having an abortion, the more she realized that she couldn't go through with it. "We'll just have to get married," she told Roy. "Besides, I want this baby."

Roy couldn't understand her. "You're only a baby yourself," he said.

When Sandy said she thought it was time to tell her mother about the baby, Roy agreed that perhaps Sandy was right. They should get married. But they wouldn't have enough money for a place of their own for a while. Sandy would need to continue living with her mother, and Roy would live with his parents.

Elsie Harper reacted exactly as Sandy had predicted. She cried and moaned and asked herself again and again what she'd done to bring up such a willful, unheeding daughter. In the end, she agreed to go with them to get the marriage license, since Sandy was underage, and she would have the wedding in her apartment. The other guests were to be Roy's mother and father.

The minister at Elsie's church performed the wedding ceremony and left immediately afterward. Elsie was a little miffed that he wouldn't stay long enough to sample the Lady Baltimore cake she'd baked for the occasion. Roy thought champagne would be the thing, but Elsie didn't believe in spirits of any kind. Instead she served coffee and lemonade. After the refreshments, Roy gave Sandy a peck on the check, rolled his eyes when Elsie wasn't looking, and followed his parents upstairs.

Sandy ranked fifth in her class when she graduated in early June. The day following commencement exercises, James McGuire was born one month prematurely by Cesarian section.

Even though the baby looked like a wizened little old man to Sandy, she loved him at first sight. Roy wasn't quite so sure of his feelings. After two weeks in the hospital, Sandy and the baby went home to Elsie's apartment, where she took over, seldom letting even Sandy hold little Jimmy. She was clearly suspicious of Roy and complained each time he came near the baby.

Roy found the situation intolerable. After a long search, he found a one-room efficiency nearby and the three McGuires moved in. When the baby was a year old, Sandy got a job as a clerk at Marshall Field's. Each morning she dropped Jimmy off with her mother on her way to work. Elsie went on the night shift at the packing plant in order to be with the baby during the day.

Remembering those years made Sandy happy and sad. She was happy for the good that had happened, and sad because those days had ended. *What happened to us?* she asked herself. *We were getting along so well.* Roy was going to night school at the University of Chicago, working toward a degree in business administration. And he managed their money so well. They seemed to have more to spend than their combined incomes would indicate. Roy was amazing. But in looking back, she could see that Roy wasn't nearly as happy as she was. He hated their little apartment, their used car they'd paid off in two years. He was always talking about moving to a suburb, Highland Park maybe, and sending Jimmy to private school. She never really understood what drove him.

Sandy looked at her watch and sighed. It was time to dress to go out to dinner with a man she hardly knew and didn't care to know any better. How could life have gone so wrong?

* * *

Everyone in the Oak Room watched as the headwaiter led Bob and Sandy to their table. Bob nodded and spoke to the people he knew, but Sandy, who didn't expect to see a familiar face, held her head high and looked straight ahead.

They were seated in the center of the room. Bob made his selections from the wine list and Sandy tried to maintain her composure. Bob asked if she was comfortable. "Not exactly," Sandy answered. "I feel conspicuous."

"You shouldn't," Bob said. "You move like a queen. I'm proud of you and proud to be seen with you."

He's a nice man, Sandy thought. *But I wish he wouldn't say those things. He embarrasses me.* To change the subject, she asked how his day had gone. "Slowly," Bob said. "I could hardly wait for seven o'clock so I could see you again."

The evening wasn't going at all the way Sandy would like. Bob was pleasant, attractive, perhaps too attentive, but she could enjoy being with him if he'd drop his wolf act. As she searched for the words to express her feelings, Bob leaned toward her. "Sandy, I don't want to waste anymore time. I can't think of anything or anyone but you. I want to marry you."

Startled, Sandy studied Bob's face. Surely he was joking. But his eyes searched hers anxiously. Suddenly she wanted to laugh. "Bob! How can you say that? We don't even know each other."

Bob flushed and looked away. Sandy thought, *I've embarrassed him, and that's the last thing I want to do.* "I'm sorry, Bob. But this is a bad time for me. Right now I have nothing to give to anyone . . . not even to my little boy."

"I can understand that," Bob said slowly. "But let

me take care of you. I can give you a home, peace of mind."

Sandy shook her head. "No, Bob. I don't want what you have to give." She paused, thinking. "It should be clear to you that I'm not myself. Any woman in her right mind would grab you, an attractive young doctor with a future. But I'm not in my right mind."

Bob grinned. "At least I tried. And now I'll bide my time. By the way, I know of a job that might interest you. How would you like to work in a bookstore?"

"Sounds good," Sandy said. "Can you tell me something about it?"

Bob explained that his sister Penny still owned the Wade Bookstore in Oakdale. And even though he hadn't heard from his sister, he told Sandy that Penny had asked him to find a new clerk for the store. Of course Penny would be delighted when she met Sandy, Bob told himself. "We'll drive by Wade's on the way back to the Stewarts'," he said.

With the prospect of a good job, Sandy's spirits rose. For the first time in two years, she could believe in the future. Now she'd find a nice apartment and she'd make a real home for Jimmy.

Chapter Four

A Change of Heart and Mind

Chris and Nancy Hughes could see that Bob was changing in certain ways. For one thing he bought a new suit and several neckties. Nancy was pleased. For months she'd been fussing at him about the way he dressed. She even went so far as to tell him he was looking "downright seedy." Chris thought Bob had a better attitude about things in general. He laughed more.

Even Tom noticed. He told Nancy, "Daddy and I have a lot of fun together."

Nancy was mystified until she had lunch with Claire Cassen a few weeks after the Stewart dinner party. After Claire had complained about Doug's working such long hours, how tired he looked, and how she worried about him, the conversation turned to children. Nancy told Claire about the changes for the better in Bob's outlook. "And lately he's been making a number of phone calls. I don't know why, but I think he's calling a woman."

Claire said, "I wouldn't be at all surprised."

Nancy was bubbling. "So I keep hoping it's Lisa he's talking to. It would be marvelous if they could get back together again."

"Don't get your hopes up, Nancy," Claire said. "I might as well tell you. Bob met a friend of Ellen's the other night. A stunning young divorcée from Chicago. I could see that Bob was quite smitten with her."

"Oh." Nancy sighed. "Well, who is she? Bob didn't mention a thing."

Claire told Nancy everything she knew about Sandy. She also reported that Doug believed that Sandy's imprisonment was a miscarriage of justice.

"I do hope so," Nancy said. "The poor thing! But I wonder if she's at all suitable for Bob. Do you know anything about her family?"

"No, I don't," Claire answered. "She has a mother who lives in Chicago. I understand she's a rather ordinary but decent person."

"Oh, dear!" Nancy was troubled. "What about the former husband?"

"He's still in prison. Oh, yes, I forgot to mention the woman has a child. A boy, I think."

Nancy forced a smile. "None of this sounds too promising, does it? I believe I'll hold the thought that this young woman is just a passing fancy."

"I'm sure that's just what she is," Claire said brightly. "Have you heard from Penny recently?"

Nancy and Claire spoke no more of Sandy. Even so, Nancy couldn't put Ellen's friend out of her mind. That night, after Tom was in bed, Nancy told Chris about Sandy. She thought he should be prepared for the changes in their lives this beautiful stranger might bring.

A few days later Nancy stopped in Wade's to buy

something new to read to Tom. As she looked through the children's books section, she heard someone say, "May I help you?"

Nancy looked up into the smiling face of a lovely young woman. "Yes, thank you. I'm looking for books to read to my grandson. I'm getting tired of reading the same stories to him over and over. But he doesn't tire of them. He's insatiable."

"How old is he?" Sandy asked.

"He's four, but unusually mature for his age."

"I know what you mean," Sandy said. "My little boy is seven, going on thirty."

At the mention of a little boy, Nancy became attentive. "Then your little boy must be in school. Which elementary school does he attend?"

"He's in school in Chicago. But he'll be going to school here in Oakdale very soon. I hope!"

"Then you must be new in Oakdale. I was just thinking that I'd never seen you in Wade's before. Evidently you haven't been working here long."

"Does it show?" Sandy asked.

Now Nancy was positive that this was the girl Claire had mentioned. Before she could say more, Sandy said, "I'll leave you to browse. If you need me, please call."

Nancy made her selections and went to the cashier's desk, hoping to see the new clerk again. But the manager waited on her and Nancy left the bookstore nagged by a number of unanswered questions. Of course, she could ask Bob about this young woman, or should she wait until he mentioned her?

For her part, Sandy had no particular interest in the pleasant, well-dressed matron she'd just waited on. This was only her first week on the job. So far the routine was a little strange to her, and she was not yet familiar with the stock in the store. After her encounter with Nancy, Sandy returned to the back room, where she was unpacking a new shipment of books.

During her lunch hour, Sandy planned to call about an apartment she'd seen listed in the real estate section of the paper. Even though Ellen kept insisting that she stay with the Stewarts until she found a place that suited her exactly, Sandy was eager to get settled.

After work that day, Sandy looked at the apartment. It wasn't bad, even though there was only one bedroom and the rent was more than she could afford. She thought quickly. Jimmy could have the bedroom, and she'd get a sofa bed for the living room and sleep on that. She was sure Mama could lend her enough money to pay the first two months' rent on the apartment and to make a down payment on some furniture. She'd take the apartment!

Ellen was delighted to see Sandy so happy. She hoped that Sandy wasn't getting in too deep financially, but didn't mention her concern.

The next few weeks seemed to drag for Sandy. She couldn't wait to get settled in the new apartment, but everything took so long! Mama had agreed to help her financially, but she was doing everything in her power to keep Jimmy with her.

"All his friends are here," Mama kept saying. "And how can you even think of changing schools in the middle of the year!"

Sandy thought Mama was being silly and overly possessive. Children were adaptable, weren't they? And Mama must come and visit them often.

Ellen did everything she could to help Sandy get settled. So did Bob. In fact, he wanted to buy the rug for Sandy's living room, but she wouldn't hear of it.

She didn't want to be beholden to him, and always, in the back of her mind, was the hope that Roy would come back one day and the three of them could be a real family again.

When the time finally came for Sandy to go after Jimmy, she rejected Ellen's offer to drive her. "The train will do nicely," she said. And although she didn't tell Ellen, Sandy was a little nervous about seeing Jimmy again. What if he wouldn't accept her? After the two-year separation, she was a stranger to him. During her brief visit in Chicago after she was released from prison, Jimmy seemed ill at ease with her. He was always saying, "Mama, may I go out and play now?" But when he said "Mama" he wasn't talking to her. In fact, he didn't call her anything! Sandy couldn't wait to get things straightened out between them.

Sandy reached her mother's apartment late on a Friday night. She peeked in at Jimmy and knew he was pretending to be asleep. He didn't want to see her! *In time*, she thought. *As soon as he gets to know me again, he'll accept me.*

On Sunday morning, as they were preparing to leave, Elsie told Sandy she wouldn't go with them to the station. She'd just tell them goodbye in the apartment. Sandy kissed her mother, saying, "Thanks, Mama, for everything. I wish you were coming with us." As she started to the door, Jimmy grabbed his grandmother around the waist. His face was ashen and his eyes were tightly closed. She knelt and held him to her, murmuring, "Now now, there now . . ."

For a moment, Sandy faltered. What was she doing to Jimmy and Mama? Could she match the love Mama had given him? She touched Jimmy's shoulder. "Come on, honey. We'll have to hurry—the taxi's waiting." As she pushed him through the doorway, she couldn't look at her mother.

They rode to the station in silence. Jimmy never looked at Sandy once until they were settled on the train and traveling toward Oakdale. "How about some lunch?" Sandy asked. "The dining car's open."

"Yes, ma'am."

When their food came, Jimmy hardly touched his. He stared out the window, keeping his head turned away so she couldn't see his face. Once he dabbed at his cheek with his napkin. Sandy wanted to hold him close and tell him everything would be wonderful. But she'd only embarrass him, and he wouldn't believe her anyway.

Rain was falling when they got off the train in Oakdale. Sandy hoped things might be better when they got home. But once inside the new apartment, the little rooms seemed cold and cheerless. Sandy knew Jimmy hated it. She bustled about, opening a can of soup and making a cheese sandwich for Jimmy. She wasn't hungry at all.

Before they sat down to eat, Jimmy said, "Miss, may I turn on the television?"

"Of course, honey." At last he'd said something to her!

Jimmy ate all of his soup, placed his napkin beside his plate, and stood up. "Thank you," he said. "If it's all right, Miss, I think I'll go to bed now."

"Of course you may go to bed!" She was tired too. And why was he being so stiff and distant? "Don't call me 'Miss'! I'm your mother—you could call me that."

"I know." The blue-gray eyes, so like Roy's, stared into hers. Then he turned and walked out of the room.

Sandy took a deep breath. This was going to take time. A lot of time. She wondered if she could ever bridge her two year absence. That, plus all the earlier years when she'd let her mother take over Jimmy's upbringing, was making her son treat her like a stranger.

She wondered if he would ever forgive her.

Now that Nancy had been alerted to Sandy's presence in Oakdale, she watched Bob for indications that he was "seeing someone." But as the days passed and Bob failed to mention Sandy to Nancy and Chris, Nancy grew more alarmed. Should she just come right out and ask him about this woman, or should she bide her time and wait for him to say something?

One evening as Bob was preparing to leave the house, Nancy blurted out, "Will you be seeing Mrs. McGuire?"

Bob was startled. "Yes I will, Mom. Tell me, how did you hear about her?"

"Half the people I know have mentioned her to me. It's a little embarrassing, not knowing anything about the woman. Yet you're constantly being seen with her."

"Oh, Mom, I haven't seen her that much. Not nearly as often as I'd like to."

"I'd like to meet her," Nancy said, hoping she didn't sound as grim as she felt.

"Fine! I'll bring her around sometime, if she'll come. She's pretty cagey. Doesn't want to get involved."

"I've heard that one before." *She's very clever,* Nancy thought. *She'll let Bob chase her until she catches him.*

"I'm trying to win her over. But so far, no luck at all." Bob kissed Nancy's cheek. "I'll bring her by sometime and let you and Dad go to work on her. You're much more charming than I am. See you later." And he was out the door.

"Did you hear that, Chris?" Nancy called.

"No, dear. I'm afraid I wasn't listening," Chris answered.

"Well, both of us had better be paying attention. One morning we may wake up to find that Bob has married this girl!"

"I think Bob *should* marry again."

"Oh, Chris!" Nancy stalked into the kitchen. For the past year, she'd been hoping that Bob and Lisa would get back together. Just think what that would do for Tommy! She would miss him so! On the other hand, it would be such a waste if Bob and Lisa didn't remarry. And now that Lisa was older and more mature, surely she'd be a good wife and mother.

Bob buzzed Sandy's apartment from the entrance hall. He heard a click but no voice. "It's Bob," he said into the speaker and the door into the vestibule opened. When he pressed the doorbell, Jimmy opened the door. "Hey, Sandy, he's here," he said and ran into his room.

Sandy appeared, smiling. "Please forgive Jimmy's manners, Bob." She made a face and said in a low voice, "We have our problems."

"The problems of the single parent!" Bob said. "Believe me, I understand too well. Tom thinks it's my fault that Lisa left. He may be right." Bob shrugged. "But I don't seem able to make it up to him, no matter how I try."

"It's the same with me," Sandy said. "Jimmy is angry because I was away from him for two years. He thinks I deserted him. And he blames me for Roy too. I don't think I can win."

"Why don't we join forces?" Bob reached out to Sandy but she fled across the room.

"Jimmy!" Sandy smiled brightly. "Won't you please come in and meet a friend of mine?" After a wait, she said with greater conviction, "Jimmy!" Jimmy came back into the room. "Dr. Hughes, my son, James McGuire."

Bob extended his hand. "I'm glad to meet you, Jimmy."

Jimmy said something under his breath.

"I didn't hear you, Jimmy," Sandy said.

"I said, Are you moving in here too?" Jimmy almost shouted the words.

Sandy put her hand over her eyes and Bob said, "No, Jimmy, I'm not. I'm going to take your mother out to dinner. But sometime soon I'd like you to meet my son."

For the first time, Jimmy looked at Bob with interest. "How old is your boy?"

"He's quite a bit younger than you. Tom is four."

"A baby!" As Jimmy started out of the room again, he called over his shoulder, "Hey, Sandy, I'm going to watch some TV."

"That's all right, dear." Sandy turned to Bob. "I just can't get him to call me 'Mother.'"

"He'll get around to it," Bob said. "Are we ready to go?"

"The sitter lives downstairs. I'll call her." Sandy stamped her foot on the floor three times. "This usually works."

A few seconds later, there was a soft knock on the door, and the teenage baby-sitter came into the room.

Bob took Sandy to the Oak Room again. It was his favorite place to go when he was out for the evening. He recalled Lisa's reactions—she'd found it "stuffy, tiresome, and entirely unexciting." He was glad to see that Sandy enjoyed being there. At any rate, she appeared to be enjoying herself tonight. She was relaxed and, it seemed to Bob, almost happy. She talked about her job, her problems with Jimmy, people she'd gotten to know through her work. And she asked Bob about himself, his work at the hospital, how he coped with Tom, and so on. Bob was elated by the change in her. Even so, he knew better than to push for a deepening relationship at this time. If Sandy wanted to be "just pals," he could go with that for the time being.

He made a point of getting Sandy home by ten-thirty and, when he said "Good night," he didn't even touch her hand. He did have the foresight to set up another meeting, to which Sandy smilingly agreed.

Before going home, Bob stopped by the hospital to check on a patient. When he drove into the garage about midnight, he was surprised to see the lights on in the living room. Maybe something had happened to Tom! Bob almost ran into the house, where he found Nancy waiting for him in the hall. "Mom! It's late. Is everything okay?"

"Is it? You tell me."

Bob could see she'd been crying. "What's happened? Is it Tommy?"

"Then you haven't heard?"

Bob was about to lose patience. "I've heard nothing . . . seen nothing."

"Well, it was in tonight's paper and it was even on the television news." Nancy sobbed. "Lisa's married!"

"She is!" He couldn't get his breath. He'd better say something. "Well, good for Lisa. Who's the pigeon?"

"Bob! What a way to talk!" Nancy felt a lot better. Bob was taking this very well. She picked up the *Tribune* and began to read. " 'Hotel Tycoon Portman Beasley Weds.' That's the headline. And look at this. It's a picture of Lisa and not very good."

Bob took the paper from Nancy. "Good enough for her! I'll be damned! She's hooked a live one this time. I wonder if she's number six or number seven."

"Seven, I believe." Nancy took the paper from Bob's hands. "It says, 'Mr. Beasley's first wife was socialite Elinor Ramsey. Then he married Candida Mallory, Fritzi Devere—'"

"Mom, spare me! The old boy must be close to seventy. But he's met his nemesis at last. Good luck to both of them."

"That's what I say, darling. Though I am bitterly disappointed in Lisa. And it's a shame for Tommy. I just hope he doesn't hear about this."

"He won't hear it from me, Mom. And I imagine it will all be over soon. And one good thing, I can stop making alimony payments."

Nancy smiled. "You know, dear, I've been thinking. Why don't you invite Mrs. McGuire to dinner here? And maybe she'll bring her little boy. Your father and I would like to meet both of them."

"Sounds good," Bob said slowly. "I'll ask her tomorrow. And it might be a good thing if you called her too."

"I'll do that. Leave me her number and I'll call her tomorrow evening." Nancy's enthusiasm was growing. "And I think I'll ask Ellen and David and Claire and Doug. What do you think, Bob?"

"I'd cool it on Claire and Doug. I don't think Sandy feels too easy around Claire."

"Whatever you say! Good night, dear." She paused and turned back to Bob on her way up the stairs. "And, Bob, I'm so glad that you're taking Lisa's marriage so well. She never was good enough for you."

When he was alone, Bob picked up the paper and studied Lisa's picture. She looked wide-eyed and startled. *Must be the flash*, Bob thought. Why would she marry a man old enough to be her grandfather?

Was it the money? Or was she a lost soul without Tom and him? Not likely. Whatever her reasons, she'd cleared the way for him to marry Sandy. That is, if Sandy would have him!

But what about Tom and that smart-aleck kid of Sandy's? Would they get along? Probably not. At least not at first. And he'd better change his attitude. Sandy's son was unhappy, rather than smart-aleck. The poor little guy had been through a lot. And if Bob could talk Sandy into marrying him, he'd be the father of two boys! The idea made him a little uncomfortable. If there would be trouble between the boys, he'd put his money on Tom any day. His son could take care of himself!

Chapter Five
Family Matters

Sandy was waiting on a customer when Bob telephoned the following morning. She was embarrassed and annoyed. He was putting her on the spot by calling her at work. She'd ask him not to do that again.

When he explained that his mother was inviting her to dinner, she replied in a curt, businesslike manner. "That will be fine. Thank you very much." When he suggested that she bring Jimmy, she said, "Sorry, that won't be possible." What a thought! She couldn't imagine what Jimmy would do in a formal situation. No way!

Bob put down the phone, feeling a little hurt. This had to be the coldest, most hardheaded female he'd ever met. Why was he wasting his time on her? But he knew the answer. He couldn't get her out of his mind, her slow smile, the gentleness he sometimes saw in her eyes, his longing to take her in his arms.

The dinner party was the following Saturday night. Bob picked Sandy up at seven and drove her to his parents' house. They arrived shortly after Ellen and David, and that was a lucky thing. Being with Ellen put Sandy at ease. Nancy and Chris found her charming, beautiful, and intelligent, and made no effort to hide their feelings. Bob was proud.

Until the last minute Sandy had tried to think of a reasonable excuse to cancel. She had no reason to meet Bob's parents. Their friendship was going nowhere—she'd see that it didn't. Of course she'd enjoy an evening with Ellen and David. With Bob's parents she intended to maintain a cordial distance. She didn't expect to see Tom.

As the guests were returning to the living room after dinner, Sandy saw Tom on the stairway, looking between the banisters. "Well, hello," she said. "Who are you?"

"I'm Tom." He padded down the stairs and hurled himself at Sandy. She picked him up.

"Who are you?" Tom said.

"I'm Sandy." She kissed his cheek.

"Hey, fella," Bob said, "a gentleman doesn't come downstairs in his night attire."

Tom ignored his father. "Is Sandy really your name?"

"It's really Alessandra. But no one calls me that."

"I do." He saw Nancy heading his way and jumped to the floor. "Good night, Alessandra," he called as he scooted back up the stairs.

Sandy turned to Bob, her eyes glowing. "He's great!"

"Thank you," Bob said, trying to avoid Nancy's eyes. When he did glance at his mother, she was still smiling with pleasure. He hoped she wasn't getting her hopes up. He planned to stay cool.

Later when he took Sandy to her door, Bob suggested that they plan an outing with their boys. Sandy hesitated. "Let's think about it."

Bob gave her a friendly peck on the cheek and left. On the way home, he reviewed the events of the evening and decided things had gone well, considering. And she didn't say no to an outing with the boys.

Nancy thought Sandy was lovely and told Bob that in detail the next morning at breakfast. Chris was more restrained. He said, "A very attractive young woman, Bob. I like her."

Bob became much busier at the hospital and didn't have free time at night. Even so he did manage to call Sandy now and then, but never during her working hours at the bookstore. Several times they discussed getting together with their boys. Sandy admitted that she was almost afraid to make plans because she didn't know how Jimmy would behave. Bob thought everything would work out nicely.

Finally there was one Saturday when Bob could see his way clear to being away from the hospital for the afternoon. He called Sandy and on the spur of the moment, she agreed. They'd take the boys to a Saturday matinee at a neighborhood movie house.

Shortly before two that afternoon, Bob, with Tom at his side, knocked on Sandy's door. Jimmy opened it immediately. "Sandy, they're here!"

Sandy rushed into the room to greet them. "Hello, Bob. And Tom!" she said, taking his hand. "How wonderful to see you!"

Tom gazed up into her face. "Alessandra, you're so pretty."

Jimmy stepped in front of Sandy, facing Tom. "She's my mother and you keep away from her." He grabbed Sandy's arm and tried to pull her away. "Come on, Mother! Let's stay here. We don't want to go to any old movie with them!"

Sandy put her arms around Jimmy and held him close. "All right, sweetie," she said softly. She turned to Bob and her eyes were glistening with tears. "Do you mind?"

"Of course not," Bob said gruffly. "We'll make it another day." He took Tom's hand and they left.

As they were getting into the car, Tom asked, "Why won't Alessandra and her boy go to the movies with us?"

Bob didn't answer for a moment. Then he said, "It's the first time Jimmy has called her Mother."

"Oh," Tom said, but he was puzzled.

Bob and Tom went to the matinee anyway. Afterward, they stopped in a coffee shop for ice cream and chatted about the film they'd just seen. Then Tom abruptly changed the subject. "Is Alessandra going to be my new mother?"

Bob took a sip of his coffee. "Why do you ask that, Tom?"

"I just thought you'd get me a new mother."

Bob was startled. "Where did you hear that?"

Tom appeared to be concentrating on shaping the ice cream with his spoon. "Somebody told me."

"Who told you that?"

"I don't remember. Well, is she?"

"Is she what?"

"Is Alessandra going to be my new mother?"

Bob winked at him. "Do you think we should ask her?"

Tom tried to wink back. "Let's," he whispered.

To Bob, the situation with Sandy wasn't promising. The woman had personal problems and a sullen, unpleasant child. Maybe he'd better back off a bit. He decided not to call her for a while. But as he and Tom were entering the house he heard Nancy say, "He's just come in, Sandy. So nice talking to you." She handed the phone to Bob.

The sound of Sandy's voice erased all his doubts. She'd called to apologize and she hoped that Bob understood why she had decided not to go. Of course he understood! She thought they should try a similar excursion in the near future. So they made a date for the following Saturday.

As the days passed, Bob's misgivings returned. The thought of Saturday filled him with dread. He wondered what Jimmy would do this time.

Sandy and Jimmy were waiting when Bob knocked at her door. Sandy walked into the hall with Jimmy right behind her. *So far, so good*, Bob thought.

When they got to the car, Bob held the door to the front seat for Sandy and opened the back for Jimmy. Jimmy glared at Tom, who had waited in the car. "Do I have to sit with the baby?"

"Jimmy, you may sit with Tom," Sandy said with firmness. Jimmy crawled into the back seat and sat with his arms folded and his eyes deliberately shut.

As he drove, Bob occasionally glanced into the rear-view mirror. Tom was trying to talk to Jimmy, but Jimmy was ignoring him. In a low voice, Bob said to Sandy, "Let's pay no attention to them and see what they do."

Sandy answered, "That's fine with me. Anyway I'm afraid to watch."

Bob tried to carry on a conversation, but couldn't keep his eyes from the rearview mirror. He was concerned when he saw Tom poke Jimmy's arm, but forced himself to look away and concentrate on finding a place to park. As he was backing into a space, there was the sound of flesh hitting flesh and a loud yowl. As Bob braked, he heard Sandy say,

"Jimmy, did you hit Tommy?"

"He was bugging me," Jimmy said.

"That's no excuse," Sandy said sharply. "He's smaller than you!"

Tom was crying and his new blue turtleneck was splattered with blood. "Daddy," he sobbed, "he hit me on the nose!"

Bob whipped the handkerchief from his breast pocket and handed it to Tom. "Here, use this! And keep your head back." The front end of the car protruded into the left lane, and the driver behind him was honking his horn. "Oh, hell!" Bob said and pulled back into the traffic. "We're all going home. Maybe we'll try this some other day!"

Sandy shrank away from him, saying nothing. Bob stopped in front of Sandy's building, and she was out of the car before he could turn off the ignition.

"Don't bother coming up with us." Sandy kept her eyes on Jimmy as he scrambled out of the car and ran to the building entrance.

"I'll call you," Bob said

Sandy gave him an icy smile and didn't answer.

Bob called Sandy from the hospital that night. A baby-sitter answered, saying that Sandy was out for the evening. Bob didn't blame her for going out. She probably wanted to get away from that brat kid of hers.

He called again two hours later. Surely she'd be home by now, tomorrow was a work day for her. This time Sandy answered.

"When can I see you?" Bob asked.

"I don't know," she answered.

Bob tried to sound casual. "Just name a day . . . an hour . . ." When she didn't answer, he could feel his head throbbing. "I think you owe me that much,

Sandy." Damn! He'd give anything to take back that last statement. He didn't want to play to her sense of guilt.

"I can see you tomorrow night." She laughed nervously. "But without the boys, wouldn't you say?"

"Good! I'll meet you in that little bar next to your building tomorrow night at nine." He was surprised and relieved by her promise to see him.

When Sandy finished talking to Bob, she returned to the bathroom mirror to complete the nightly ritual of cleaning and creaming her face. It was such a luxury being able to take care of her skin and use lotions. For two whole years, she couldn't do any of those things. She leaned closer to the mirror. Was she getting wrinkles around her eyes? Maybe not yet. But soon!

Maybe she should have said no when Bob wanted to meet her tomorrow night. She dreaded that. Even though Bob hadn't mentioned marriage in six months, that was what he still wanted. She looked into the bedroom at Jimmy. He was beautiful! And when he was sleeping, as he was now, he looked like an angel. The dark hair, the fine features. He was so like Roy! How could she even think of marrying Bob when she still loved Roy?

But she didn't have Roy. And she made such a little bit of money! Jimmy hated this cramped, shabby little apartment. He said he was ashamed to bring his friends home to play. But this was the best she could do. She couldn't see how she could raise Jimmy without help from someone. She couldn't keep asking Mama for money.

If she married Bob, she and Jimmy could live in a house . . . and she wouldn't need to worry about money. Bob was nice and dependable. She liked him a lot, and he was fun to be with. *But . . .*

Sandy was twenty minutes late for their nine o'clock appointment and she didn't apologize. She slipped into the booth, across from Bob, and waited for him to say something.

"Sandy!" He was almost yelling. "It's hard to talk over that." He indicated the juke box in the corner. "Would you rather go to some other place?"

Sandy shrugged. "This is fine."

Bob looked into her eyes. "I haven't asked you to marry me lately. I thought I'd better let up on that idea. But I'm asking now. Sandy, will you marry me?" A waiter approached and Bob said, "What would you like?"

"Nothing for me," Sandy said

Bob waved the waiter away and leaned toward her. "You haven't answered me, Sandy."

"Couldn't we go on just as we are?" Sandy asked in a small voice. When Bob didn't answer, her words came out in a rush. "I just don't love you, Bob. Not the way I should. And our boys will never get along. No! I can't marry you!"

Bob got to his feet, pulled several bills out of his trouser pocket, and put them on the table. "May I walk you to your door?"

"Thanks, no," Sandy said.

"Then I guess this is goodbye, Sandy. Be happy!" He walked out of the bar.

Sandy watched him go. *Everything happened too fast,* she thought. *He rushed me—we should have talked longer. Then just to walk out and leave me alone!* Everyone in the room was looking at her. What if someone said something? She hated this place. It was so dingy—just neon lights over the bar. She'd better get away and back to Jimmy and the apartment. She hurried out and ran the few steps to her building.

* * *

A few weeks later Ellen stopped by Wade's around eleven-thirty in the morning. She made her purchases and waited until Sandy was free. "Where've you been keeping yourself?" Ellen asked. "I haven't seen you in ages. Could we have lunch?"

"I only have thirty minutes," Sandy said. "Wait until I get my coat. Would you mind going to the sandwich shop next door?"

"How are you?" Ellen asked after they'd placed their orders. "You don't quite seem yourself."

"I'm fine," Sandy answered. "A little depressed maybe, but I'm okay. How are the boys?"

They discussed their children for a few minutes. Then Sandy said, "Have you seen Bob?"

"A few times. I gather you haven't seen him."

"No. Things got a little thick so we decided not to see each other for a while. Was he alone when you saw him?"

Ellen laughed. "No."

"I see," Sandy said quietly. "Ellen, I think I may have made a mistake."

Ellen studied Sandy. She was concerned about her. "Why don't you call him, Sandy? Bob doesn't look happy either."

"I couldn't do that. Anyway you just said he's seeing someone."

"Not someone! Everytime I've seen Bob, he's been with a different girl. Shall I tell him you asked about him?"

"Please don't do that! I'm sorry, but it's time for me to get back to work. Call me."

Before Ellen could answer, Sandy was gone. That night she told David about the conversation. "Do you think I should say something to Bob?"

"Certainly not!" David was emphatic. "You stay out of this."

"I suppose you're right," Ellen said meekly. But she wished she could do something.

For the rest of that afternoon, Sandy thought about Bob and about Ellen's suggestion that she call him. Should she or shouldn't she? Why was she so upset that Bob was seeing other women? He had every right, didn't he? Could she possibly be jealous? Maybe she was a little in love with Bob after all. By the time she'd prepared supper for Jimmy, she'd talked herself into believing she cared deeply for him. She dialed Bob's home number and waited.

On the third ring, he answered, "Dr. Hughes."

Sandy could hardly get the words out. "Uh, Bob? This is . . ."

"Sandy! Are you all right?"

"Yes. Of course."

"Are you at home?"

"Yes," Sandy answered.

"I'll be right over."

Sandy put down the telephone and collapsed on the sofa. That was fast! Now what had she gotten herself into?

Jimmy was watching her from the kitchen doorway. "Are you going to marry Bob Hughes?"

"I don't know," Sandy answered. "Would you care if I did?"

"Nope. Go ahead. I hate that kid of his so I just won't play with him. But Bob's okay."

Sandy smiled at him. "Thank you for your support." She looked around the tiny apartment. "And help me straighten up this place."

Within fifteen minutes, Bob was at her door. She invited him in and they stared at each other without speaking. Then Bob said, "Why don't we go for a drive?"

Bob drove out of Oakdale and into the country. Clouds covered the moon. *That's strange*, he thought. *The night was so clear thirty minutes ago.* He put his hand over Sandy's and for once she didn't draw away from him.

Bob turned off the road and into a country lane choked with weeds and stopped the car. "I love this place," he said. "Just ahead, about a hundred yards, is the old house my grandparents lived in. Someday I plan to fix it up and live here too. What do you think?"

"It's very nice," Sandy said. "But it's gotten so foggy I can barely see."

Bob put his arm around Sandy and drew her close. "Forgive me if I repeat myself, but will you marry me?"

Sandy pulled away. "Bob, there are things you should know."

"Whatever you want to tell me, I don't care. These past weeks have been awful!"

"Just listen to me!" Sandy said a little desperately. "I'm not sure I love you. I love being with you, but I don't feel romantic. Do you understand?"

"I'm not sure," Bob said slowly. "I wish you felt differently, but do you like me well enough to marry me?"

"I think so. But I still think about Roy sometimes. Does that matter?"

"And sometimes I think of Lisa," Bob said. "But not kindly. I'm conceited enough to think I can make you love me. We can make a go of marriage. I know it!" Bob kissed her then and she didn't pull away immediately.

"Is it a deal?" Bob asked.

"It's a deal," Sandy answered.

Bob started the motor. "Let's go tell the folks!"

Sandy tensed. "Do you think we should?"

"They'll be thrilled!" Bob turned the car around and sped back toward Oakdale.

"Aren't you driving a little fast?"

"Wonderful!" Bob almost shouted. "We've been engaged less than three minutes, and you're sounding like a wife."

Sandy was clutching the armrest. "It's so foggy it's hard to see where we're going."

"So it is." Bob slowed down.

With Sandy following close behind him, Bob tore into the house, calling, "Mom! Are you still up?"

Nancy appeared at the top of the stairway, fastening the clasps on her robe. "Bob dear, whatever's the matter?"

"Sandy and I are getting married!"

Nancy hurried downstairs and kissed Sandy, then Bob. "When?" She was gasping with excitement. "This is marvelous. And Tommy will be so happy!"

"We haven't set a date," Sandy said.

"But it's going to be soon!" Bob grabbed Sandy and kissed her on the mouth. "Isn't it, Sandy!"

When she could get her breath, Sandy said, "Soon."

A dreamy look came into Nancy's eyes. "And we'll give a party to announce the engagement." She hugged Sandy. "Oh, my dear, you've made me so happy!"

Chapter Six
Wedding Bells

Nancy wanted to wake Chris up and tell him the good news, but Bob said, "Now, Mom, Sandy and I will be married a long time. You can tell Dad when he wakes up in the morning."

Sandy said she had to go home right away because she had to be at work early the next morning. They left Nancy in the kitchen, making a guest list for the announcement party she and Chris would give. "I might as well be doing something worthwhile," she said. "I won't sleep a wink for the rest of the night. I'm too excited."

As he backed his car out of the driveway, Bob noticed a gray sedan parked across the street. He saw the car again when he came out of Sandy's apartment building. The lights were off, but Bob could hear the motor running and see the glow of a cigarette on the driver's side. If he hadn't been lost in plans for the future, he would have noticed that the car followed him home.

A few days later, Sandy saw someone on the street

who looked like Roy. She called to him, but the man, whoever he was, didn't stop. Sandy ran after him, but he disappeared into the crowd. *I'm being silly*, she told herself, and put the incident out of her mind.

Meanwhile Nancy was actively preparing for the announcement party. Even though she was sending invitations, she called Claire and told her of the engagement. When Claire wasn't too enthusiastic about the news, Nancy didn't mind. Claire was being Claire. But when Claire said, "Would you like me to decorate? I'll drape the sun room in black bunting," Nancy thought she was going too far and told her so.

Jimmy was happy about the engagement too. He told his friends at school, "My mom's marrying a doctor, and we're going to live in a big house and I'll have lots of toys." His friends were impressed.

During afternoon recess, Jimmy's class was in the playground. One of the boys said, "See that guy on the other side of the fence. He's watching us." Another boy said, "Maybe he wants to sell us some dope." Jimmy said nothing. He'd seen the man hanging around the schoolyard before and thought he looked like his father. If that was who he was, he didn't want the guys to know. And he didn't want his mother to know either.

As he walked home from school that afternoon, Jimmy knew the man was following him. He wanted to get a close look at the guy! Leaving his friends at Elm Street, he turned the corner and flattened himself against the side of the brick building, the way he'd seen TV detectives do, and waited for his pursurer.

He didn't have long to wait. Roy turned the corner, and Jimmy grabbed his arm. "Is that you, Daddy?"

Roy was caught off guard. He stopped and looked down into Jimmy's face. "Jimmy," he whispered. "Son!

How are you?"

"I'm fine, Daddy. I thought it was you, but I wasn't sure. Why did you wait so long to speak to me?"

"I'll explain later," Roy said. "How's your mother?"

"Fine. Are you going to come live with us?"

Roy studied Jimmy's face. "Do you want me to?"

"Yeah." Jimmy avoided Roy's eyes. "Sure I do, Dad."

"Do you think your mom wants me?"

Jimmy was beginning to fidget. "Why don't you ask her? Uh, Dad, I have to go home now."

"I'll walk part of the way with you," Roy said, and the two walked hand in hand toward the apartment.

"Daddy, did you miss me while you were away?"

"I sure did," Roy answered.

"Then why did you stay away from me so long?"

"Did your mom tell you where I was?"

"She said you were working for some people and when you finished the job, you might come back."

"And that's just what happened," Roy said. "I finished the job and here I am. I hear your mom's getting married."

"Yeah. That's what she said." Jimmy began to wish his father would go away again.

"Do you like the man she's going to marry?"

"Dr. Hughes? He's okay, I guess. He's rich!"

Roy stopped walking and reached for Jimmy's other hand. "I want you to promise me something, son," he said. "Promise you won't tell Mom you saw me!"

As Jimmy hesitated, Roy repeated, "Promise!"

"Promise," Jimmy said softly.

Roy hugged him once more and hurried away.

Jimmy had no appetite that night, and Sandy was worried. She felt his forehead. "I don't think you have a fever. I hope you aren't getting something."

"I'm okay, Mom," Jimmy said. He felt guilty though.

Should he tell her? He'd promised not to, but he was sure she'd like to know. He decided to go to bed earlier than usual. That way Mom wouldn't bug him and he'd have a better chance of keeping his promise.

The night of the announcement party, Bob picked Sandy up an hour before the guests were expected. As he turned into the driveway, he noticed a gray sedan parked across the street. He hoped there'd be enough parking space for the expected guests. "Do you know how many people Mom has invited?" he asked.

"I saw the list, but I didn't know many of them." Sandy was dreading the evening. All those strangers looking her over, wondering if she were good enough for Bob Hughes.

Bob came around to her side of the car to open the door for her. "Courage! Remember, it'll all be over by midnight." He took her hand to help her out of the car and they strolled into the house.

By ten the party was at its height. Even Sandy was having a good time—she knew more of the guests than she'd expected. She was sorry that Mama hadn't come, but maybe it was for the best. Mama might have felt uncomfortable in this crowd. Sandy chatted with Ellen and David, with the girls she worked with at Wade Bookstore, and with Claire and Doug.

Claire was on her best behavior. Sandy had never seen her in this mood before and was even beginning to like her. Then Doug got a call from the hospital and, after making brief apologies, he left.

Claire turned to Sandy. "Now pay attention to me! Marry a doctor and you'll always go home alone. There's still time. Get out of this marriage now!" She laughed and after a moment, Sandy laughed too.

Sandy heard the doorbell. *More guests*, she thought. Nancy and Chris had an amazing number of friends.

Out of the corner of her eye, she saw Chris leave a group of people and go into the hall. Michael Shea, a resident at Memorial Hospital, had joined her and Claire, and Sandy was trying to remember what Bob had said about him.

Chris was back in the room with his impassive lawyer face. Now Bob was talking to Chris, and both of them left the room. Something must be wrong, Sandy decided.

Now Bob was at her side, saying, "Pardon us, Claire, Michael." Bob's arm was around her waist as he guided her through the dining room and into the hall. She couldn't believe it. There was Roy! She called his name and ran toward him, but he stepped backward and looked away from her. Why couldn't he look her in the eye? "Roy! What are you doing here?"

"Am I a nasty surprise, Sandy?"

"You know damn well you are. What are you doing here, McGuire?" Bob asked.

Chris put his hand on Bob's arm. "Take it easy, son."

Roy squared his shoulders. "I've come to fetch my wife."

Sandy began to cry. "Roy, Roy, I don't understand. Why are you doing this?"

"I've come back for you, Sandy," Roy said gently. "I want you and Jimmy with me. We'll go back to Chicago and start over."

Roy seemed different, Sandy thought. He looked so small and thin. And he wouldn't look into her eyes. She couldn't recognize the expression in those pale blue, cold eyes.

Chris said, "Sandy may do as she sees fit. But she's under absolutely no obligation to you. You have no legal claim. The divorce has been final for over a year."

"The divorce has nothing to do with anything.

Sandy's my wife and Jimmy's my son. I'm taking them with me."

Sandy couldn't think. This man wasn't the Roy she knew. He scared her.

"Sandy, will you let me handle this?" Bob said.

Sandy couldn't look at Roy. She took Chris's arm, and they went back down the hall. As they reached the stairway, Sandy pulled away from Chris and ran upstairs.

Bob turned to Roy. "Let's talk outside." He led Roy through the sun room to the side entrance and out onto the patio. "How long have you been in town, McGuire?"

"About a week. Long enough!"

"You've been following me, haven't you?"

"Now and then."

"And why have you waited until tonight to make yourself known?"

Roy lit a cigarette and inhaled before he spoke. "Just wanted to study the setup. Find out if Sandy has changed."

"I see," Bob said quietly. "You weren't sure you wanted her back?"

"You're making things too simple, Doc. There's a hell of a lot more to it. But I don't think you'd understand."

"Try me," Bob said.

"I've been on the inside long enough to be scared out here. I'm not sure I can handle things . . . make a living anymore. How am I going to feed a wife and a kid?"

"Do you have a job?"

"No. And I'm running out of cash. Then when I heard Sandy was going to marry you, I had to make my move. I won't let her marry anybody else."

"I'm sorry for you, McGuire," Bob said. "I don't think you really want Sandy and Jimmy, yet you don't want to let them go."

Bob paused, thinking he heard the side door open. Was that Sandy? He turned to look, but saw no one. "I can give Sandy love, security, a home. And I can do a lot for Jimmy. Give him a good start in life, an education. And I'll love him too."

"You're making a piker out of me, Doc!" Roy dropped his cigarette and ground it under his heel.

"I don't mean to do that," Bob said. "But I don't believe you want Sandy. If you did, you'd have gone to her immediately. You wouldn't have skulked around, spying on her."

"I tried to explain that," Roy said lamely.

"I'll make you a deal, Roy," Bob said slowly. "I'll write you a check for fifteen thousand. That should keep you going until you find a job. And you can take care of Sandy and your boy. If you can persuade Sandy to go with you, I lose. If she turns you down, I win. How about it?"

Roy shrugged. "I'll accept your deal. But you're a fool, Hughes."

"Wait here and I'll bring the check." Bob went back into the house and through the darkened sun room.

Roy watched him leave and then relaxed in a lawn chair. When Bob returned, he stood and took the check. "Thanks, Doc," he said. "Now I'm going to tell you something worth a lot more to you than fifteen thousand is to me. Forget Sandy. She's not for you. So long!" He walked across the lawn and was out of sight.

Bob waited until he heard the car start and get underway before he went back into the house. Within a few hours, Sandy would make her decision to go with Roy or stay with him. There wasn't a thing he could do now. He might as well rejoin the party.

He walked into the living room, and Sandy was at his side.

"Where's Roy?"

"He left." Bob watched Sandy for a reaction.

"Good! Excuse me, Bob. I must mingle." She gave him a dazzling smile and left to thread her way through the crowd to speak with Ellen.

Bob watched in amazement. She was poised, beautiful, and untouched. How did she do it? He remembered Roy's parting comment and wondered what he meant. Probably nothing more than sour grapes, Bob decided.

Not long afterward, the party broke up and the guests left. Nancy collapsed on the sofa, declaring the evening a great success. Sandy was unusually talkative. She'd "had a wonderful time!" Chris was more quiet than usual, Bob thought. For that matter, he didn't have a lot to say either. But neither Nancy nor Sandy seemed to notice.

Bob thought Sandy would want to discuss Roy and what had happened on the drive back to her apartment. But she didn't.

"Please, Bob," she said, "let's not talk about Roy tonight. Maybe we should never talk about him. Do you mind?"

He took Sandy to her door and would have liked to go in for a few minutes. But Sandy said, "I'm so tired and it's so late. It's been a wonderful evening, but I must get some sleep." She kissed him on the cheek and shut the door. Bob walked slowly down the stairs and back to his parked car, wondering how soon Sandy would hear from Roy. And when she did hear, what would she do?

Sandy went into the bedroom to check on Jimmy.

Thank God! He was sleeping like an angel. She bent to kiss him lightly on the forehead and returned to the living room.

She was too upset to sleep. That bastard Roy! He'd sold out for fifteen thousand dollars! Sold her and Jimmy. Knowing Roy as she did, he could have been bought for less. And Bob was a fool! Was fifteen thousand the value he placed on her? But she was the biggest fool of all. If Roy had come to her six hours ago, she'd have followed him anywhere he chose to go.

It was a good thing she'd gone into the sun room to hear them haggling over her. Now she knew exactly what they thought of her. Maybe she should have said something to let them know she'd heard. She could have told them off, both of them, and said things to hurt them, to pay them back.

No. She was glad she hadn't—that wouldn't have worked out at all. And what difference did it make? She didn't love Roy or Bob! The only person she really cared about was Jimmy. And herself, of course! So let them think she was a dumb nothing. She'd never see Roy again, but she needed Bob. He could give her and Jimmy everything they wanted, and they'd take everything he had to offer.

Suddenly Sandy felt better. For the first time in her life, she was in control. From now on she was going to call the shots. She yawned and stretched. She could feel the tensions slipping away. Maybe she could sleep after all.

Sandy called Bob at the hospital before ten the next morning. She could hear the quality of his voice change when he recognized hers. Let him think she was leaving Oakdale with Roy! After allowing him to stew for a bit, she said, "Do you think we could get married this Saturday?"

When she got tired of his enthusiasm, she said, "Sorry, I must help a customer," and put back the phone.

Nancy was happy to make the necessary arrangements for the wedding. The bride and groom were too busy to be involved, especially since Sandy, who needed something to wear, had to make a flying trip to Chicago. There in an elegant little shop on Michigan, where she established a charge account, Sandy found the perfect dress, a Dior original in russet silk.

Sandy and Bob were married in the small chapel of the Oakdale Presbyterian Church on Saturday afternoon at four. Those attending were Jimmy, Tom, Chris and Nancy Hughes, David, Ellen, Paul and Dan Stewart, Claire and Doug Cassen. But just before the service, Doug got a call from the hospital and had to leave.

The wedding was a small family-oriented affair and very nice. Knowing that she probably wouldn't have come anyway, Sandy didn't even bother to invite her mother.

After the ceremony, Sandy and Bob went directly to the airport for their flight to Bermuda. Nancy and Chris took Jimmy home to stay with them while his mother and new father were away on their honeymoon.

Chapter Seven
Problems, More Problems

Oakdale was an hour from Chicago by air. Bob wanted to fly to Chicago, spend the night there, and leave for Bermuda the next day. But Sandy wouldn't hear of it. She wanted to go directly to Bermuda.

So they flew to Chicago, changed planes for New York International Airport, and caught a 7 P.M. flight for Hamilton, Bermuda. By the time they reached their hotel, five miles out of Hamilton, Sandy was asleep on her feet. She fell into bed, blind to the luxury of the honeymoon suite and the majesty of the Atlantic, as viewed from their balcony.

Bob was unable to sleep. He lay awake until nearly dawn, listening to Sandy's even breathing, yearning to wake her up, worrying about Tom and Jimmy. Would they be too much for Nancy and Chris to handle? Then with strong sunlight on his face, he heard Sandy's cheery greeting, "Wake up, darling. Time's a-wasting." He opened one eye and groaned.

Sandy was showered and dressed in a magnificently simple linen suit for which he would soon be billed.

"Aren't you hungry, darling? I'm starved."

"Why don't we have breakfast sent up?" Bob mumbled.

"And miss the ocean view from the terrace dining room? Besides, I'm dressed."

Bob sat up. "Come here. I've hardly kissed you since the wedding."

"There's plenty of time for that." She left the bedroom, calling over her shoulder, "Come on, slow-poke. I'll meet you in the dining room."

"Damn!" Bob muttered and got out of bed.

Bob had envisioned long, lazy days of sand and sea, moonlit strolls, hand in hand, along the beach, candle-lit dinners in out-of-the way, picturesque little restaurants.

Sandy's ideas differed somewhat. She loved the little shops where perfumes, fine china, and clothing were to be had duty-free. Bob couldn't resist the way her lovely brown eyes glowed at the sight of such things, so he didn't protest.

She also loved to spend long hours on the beach without moving, soaking up the sun that turned her skin a deep bronze. By Bob's second day of sunbathing, his hide was painfully burned and he was forced to spend the next three days in their suite, doused in healing, but faintly unpleasant-smelling ointments. They did dine in two charming little out-of-the-way restaurants that had great ambience. But for the most part, Sandy preferred their hotel's dining room with its excellent orchestra and dance floor. Bob thought Sandy was by far the most beautiful woman in the room.

When they were alone, Sandy was affectionate and she loved to cuddle. She seemed to endure sex, but couldn't respond with any emotion even resembling physical passion. When the act was completed, Sandy ran to the shower. Bob could sense his own ardor lessening.

They spent happy hours planning their future, their home, the boys' futures. Bob had retained an architect to submit drawings for rebuilding his grandparents' old home. Meanwhile he thought they might live in an apartment as the house was being rebuilt.

Sandy agreed that the house was a wonderful idea for sometime in the future. But it would take too long to remodel. And there was this wonderful house that had recently come on the market. She had heard customers discuss it and was curious enough to drive past it. It had grounds and a big in-ground pool.

Bob agreed to go and see it.

And there was the matter of furniture. Bob threatened to leave that job entirely to Sandy. He didn't have the time or the know-how. Sandy had her heart set on antiques, eighteenth century, to be precise. Well, that was definitely Sandy's department. Bob knew nothing about antiques.

When the bride and groom had made their hurried departure, without so much as a grain of rice thrown at them, Nancy had an empty feeling in the pit of her stomach. "I wanted to give a little supper or something," she said to Claire.

"Then let's have a supper for ourselves," Claire said. "Doug won't be home until eleven tonight, if then! And I'm hungry. Let's eat! My party!"

David said he had to get back to the hospital, so the remaining members of the wedding party went to the Oak Room for a festive dinner.

At Claire's suggestion the four boys were seated at a separate table. "Paul and Dan can look after the two little boys," Claire said to Nancy. "This will give you a little recreation before taking over."

Nancy was worried. "I don't know, Claire. Perhaps Tom should sit beside me. Then I can order for him."

"Nonsense! Tom's going to have to start looking after himself, particularly now that he has an older brother. He must learn to cope."

"You're being naughty again, Mother," Ellen said. "Jimmy and Tom will be great company for each other."

"That's what I'm hoping, Ellen," Nancy said, but she looked worried.

The waiter said something to Claire who raised her hand in a gesture of dismissal. "Whatever," she said, and turned to Nancy. "As usual, you're dreaming. I've said nothing until now, but that Jimmy is a little demon. Give him a few years and he'll be a first-rate juvenile delinquent!"

"Mother!" Ellen turned to Nancy. "You know she doesn't mean that."

Nancy was trying to ignore Claire. Her back was to the children's table, and she hated turning around too often. Even so she felt compelled to monitor their activities as everybody ate. She wished Claire were not so thoughtless. Obviously, she was too busy tonight playing the lady of the manor.

Suddenly there were scuffling sounds and Tom shrieked, "No, no, don't . . ."

Nancy and Chris were on their feet. Jimmy was chasing Tom in and out among the tables, grasping a lobster and yelling, "Get ya! Get ya!"

It was over quickly. The maitre d' grabbed Jimmy, and Chris caught Tom. Nancy was almost in tears, and Claire was gasping with laughter.

"Really, Mother," Ellen said, "Nancy is terribly

upset. Can't you do something!"

Nancy picked up her purse and started putting on her gloves, smoothing the leather over her fingers. "Thank you so much for the dinner, Claire. But now Chris and I really must be getting home with the boys."

"I'm sorry, Nancy," Claire said. "This is all my fault. The waiter may have said that Jimmy ordered a lobster. I wasn't listening. Can you forgive me?"

"Eventually, but not now," Nancy said. "I'll call you tomorrow." Holding her head high, she left to look for Chris and the boys. She found them in the lobby. Chris was looking a little pale, she thought.

Chris said, "If you can corral these two for a minute, I'll get the car."

Nancy nodded and took each boy by the hand. "As soon as we get home, we're going to have a talk."

Jimmy looked straight ahead, and Tom leaned against her. Nancy kept a firm grasp on Jimmy's hand and counted the days until Bob and Sandy would return.

That night after Tom was asleep, Nancy went into Jimmy's room. As she had expected, she found him wide awake. "I came to kiss you good night," she said.

Jimmy glanced at her and looked away. "You don't have to."

"It's no bother. And furthermore I want to get to know you better, especially now that I'm your step-grandmother."

"Is that what you want me to call you?"

Nancy was puzzled for a second. "Oh? Why, yes, if you like."

"Okay, Step-grandmother. What do you want to know about me?"

"Just about everything," Nancy said. "Your favorite

kind of birthday cake, what you want for your birthday, uh . . . what you plan to wear on Halloween . . . lots of things."

There was a faraway look in Jimmy's eyes. "A pumpkin. A great big orange pumpkin."

Nancy was startled. "You want to masquerade as a pumpkin?" She could see Jimmy studying her, judging her. "Well, why not! That's a wonderful idea." Impulsively she leaned over and kissed his cheek. "You know, Jimmy, I think we're going to get along just fine!"

"You and me, maybe, and Chris. But I hate that crybaby kid!"

"Oh, Jimmy, I want you to like Tom."

Jimmy stared at her and then turned over and closed his eyes. "I'll try," he said.

Nancy was pleased and relieved. She switched off the light and tiptoed out of the room.

The next day Nancy talked to Tom about being kind and thoughtful to Jimmy. She went to great lengths to explain that Jimmy was away from his mother and living in an unfamiliar place with people he hardly knew. Tom didn't understand what Nancy meant by "unfamiliar." Nancy said, "He's never been in this house before. He doesn't know where things are. He needs you to show him around."

"You mean, if there's a hole in the yard, Jimmy doesn't know about it?" Tom said.

"That's exactly what I mean," Nancy said.

In trying to entertain and distract both boys, Nancy made a big event of Halloween. Tom wanted to be a black cat, and Nancy put together his costume with no great difficulty. But Jimmy's pumpkin suit was more involved. Finally, with the help of a dressmaker, the suit was constructed over a wire framework and turned out quite well. Jimmy loved it. Nancy worried that he might not be able to see to get around.

Jimmy said, "Don't worry. I can handle it, just as long as that little kid keeps out of my way."

After an early supper on Halloween, both boys were in their costumes and ready to go trick-or-treating. "Do I have to stay with this kid?" Jimmy asked Nancy.

"I believe you do, dear," Nancy said. "None of your friends from school lives in this neighborhood."

"This is going to be weird," Jimmy grumbled. "I don't know how to act with a bunch of little kids."

"Just look where you're going," Chris said.

When the boys were out of the house and on their way, Nancy went into the kitchen and poured herself a cup of coffee. "I'm going to relax and enjoy this," she told Chris. "Getting ready for Halloween is a much bigger job than having a sit-down dinner for thirty people. I do hope they have a good time."

Thirty minutes later, a policeman, with Tom in tow, rang their bell. When Chris opened the door, Tom said, "Granddad, guess what? Jimmy fell into an unfamiliar hole."

"Sorry, Mr Hughes," the officer said, "but that's exactly what happened. The children were cutting through your neighbor's backyard and . . ."

Nancy groaned. "I forgot. The Ellisons' swimming pool! They drained it last week."

"Yes, ma'am, and your other little boy fell into it. Lucky for him, he fell into the shallow end, but I'm afraid he's broken his leg."

"It's all my fault," Nancy moaned. "I shouldn't have let him go. It's so dark, and I knew he couldn't see where he was going."

"He'll be fine, ma'am. The ambulance picked him up two minutes ago and he's on his way to the hospital. They'll take good care of him."

"Oh, Chris, one of us should be with Jimmy."

"Now don't you worry, Mrs. Hughes. These young ones mend fast, you know. And this is a brave young fellow."

"Chris, you stay here with Tom. I'm going to the hospital." Nancy started to the door and stopped. "Oh, Chris, don't you think we'd better call Sandy?"

Chris thanked the officer and came back to Nancy. "Take it easy, old girl. No point in calling them tonight—they can't get a plane until morning. You stay here with Tom, and I'll go to the hospital."

Later when Nancy was putting Tom to bed, she said, "Tom, how did it happen that Jimmy fell into the Ellisons' pool and broke his leg?"

"I couldn't help it, Grandmother. I tried to tell Jimmy about the unfamiliar place, but he said I was a crybaby and didn't know anything and to keep quiet. So I did."

Nancy decided not to pursue the subject further. She might learn more than she cared to know.

Sandy and Bob were at breakfast when they received the call from Chris. "Oh, my poor baby! How could this happen?" Sandy cried.

Bob did his best to calm her. "Now, Sandy, Dad said Jimmy was just fine. He's in good spirits and he's in no pain."

But Sandy wouldn't be comforted. "I know he's suffering! We must leave immediately!"

"Try to be calm, Sandy. I'll check on the flight." Bob started to walk away.

"I know Tom hates Jimmy. I'll bet Tom pushed him!"

"What a thing to say, Sandy! Tom's five years old! That's a little young for criminal intent!" Bob put his arm around Sandy. "Don't worry. Jimmy will be fine."

Sandy turned away from him. "That's what you say! I should never have left him with strangers."

"Strangers! How can you call my family strangers?" Bob hurried to the desk to check on flights to Chicago.

Chapter Eight
Home, Unhappy Home

Tom Hughes stared across the desk at his high school guidance counselor, Mrs. Best, watching her shuffle papers. Now and then she paused to read a sentence, then turned to another page. She called him in for a conference at least once a month and always found something to chew him out about. He was only faintly curious about the topic for today.

"I was hoping one of your parents would be with you," she said. "Did you tell your mother or father I wanted to see one of them?"

What a ridiculous question! He could just see Dr. Bob, a slight frown creasing his brow, stethoscope in hand. Or Sandy! She'd never be able to make up her mind what to wear, and the hour of the appointment would pass while she wavered between the Simpson and the Dior. Mrs. Best gave him a sharp look. "No, ma'am," Tom said.

Mrs. Best muttered something that sounded like, "These people!"

Tom leaned back in his chair, considering the right

attitude for today's session. Should he be afraid, belligerent, or agreeable?

"Your grades are deplorable, Tom," Mrs. Best was saying. "Your SATs are above average, but here's an incomplete for history. And you've failed trig!" She shook her head. "Unless you make a dramatic turnaround, you won't get into a college." She looked at him, waiting for a response.

What was there to say? Tom looked away after he'd seen Mrs. Best's flush of annoyance. *I'm really getting to her,* he thought. *Now she'll try to shame me.*

"What is it with you?" Mrs. Best asked. "You come from a good family. High achievers. You live in a beautiful house—you've been given every advantage." Mrs. Best sighed heavily. "Why do I have this deep-seated feeling that I'm wasting my time?"

Tom wished she'd be quiet. He was so sleepy. He tried to make his mind go blank. The old girl couldn't care less whether or not he went to college. She probably went to some jerk-water place and what good had it done her? She was stuck with him. It was so hot in this dingy little office. He could hardly keep his eyes open. As soon as he got out of here, he'd get into the car and drive around for a while. Get some air. Now what was she saying?

"I was in your mother's bookstore yesterday. She's very charming. So intelligent, so well-informed . . ."

"Stepmother's."

Mrs. Best looked puzzled. "I beg your pardon."

"I said, she's my stepmother."

"Oh! I just assumed . . ."

"That's okay."

"And of course your father is one of the most respected . . . Uh, is your mother living?"

"I guess so. But you couldn't prove it by me. If she

died, someone might tell me—maybe."

"Where does your mother live, Tom?"

"Chicago, I guess. Who the hell knows? Uh . . . excuse me, Mrs. Best."

"You're excused." Mrs. Best smiled. "Do you think your father would stop in and talk with me?"

Persistent old bitch! He'd bet she was thirty if she was a day. He wished she'd get off his back. "I don't know, ma'am," Tom said.

Mrs. Best straightened the papers on her desk and put them in a manila folder. "That will be all for today, Tom. And for heaven's sake, hit the books!"

Tom grinned and walked out of the office.

A few minutes later, Bob Hughes answered his phone.

The caller identified herself as Tom's counselor at Oakdale High School. As she began to explain the reason for her call, David Stewart opened the door and beckoned. Bob said, "I'm sorry, Mrs. Best. May I get back to you?" He put down the phone and followed David down the hall to Doug Cassen's office.

Doug was sitting at his desk with a sheepish smile on his face. When he saw David and Bob, he said, "I felt dizzy for a second. That's all. I'm fine now."

The two men exchanged glances and David said, "Why don't we run a few tests, Doug?"

"I'm as aware of the extent of my problems as both of you are. I'm taking things easy—I've delegated responsibilities. So let's forget this episode."

"Does Claire know about all this?" Bob asked.

"No!" Doug said emphatically. "Now I have a couple of calls to make. So if you'll excuse me—" He lifted the phone and waited for them to leave.

"Aye, aye, sir," David said and left Doug's office, followed by Bob.

As they walked down the hospital corridor together, Bob said, "One of these days, Doug isn't going to survive an episode."

"And I wish he'd discuss this with Claire! I hate to think . . ." David left the thought unfinished. He stopped at the elevator bank.

"See you tonight?"

"Right!" Bob hurried back to his office. He had a patient waiting.

Bob sped up the long, curving driveway to his house and braked sharply at the entrance. As he entered the reception hall, he saw Sandy coming down the stairway. *She looks like a queen*, Bob thought. He'd never particularly cared for this house—it was too imposing—but Sandy had wanted it and the place suited her.

"Hello, dear," he said.

"I thought you weren't going to make it," Sandy greeted him. "You'd better hurry and shower. Your things are laid out on the bed. We're expected at the Stewarts' by seven-thirty."

"I'll be ready," Bob said. Damn, he'd forgotten to return that woman's call. "Is Tom home?"

"I haven't seen him. Maybe he's in the kitchen. I told Cook to leave something for him to eat."

"Thanks. I'll check."

Tom wasn't in the kitchen. Bob went to his room and found him lying on his bed, listening to loud, blasting music. Shuddering, Bob crossed the room to turn off the stereo. "How can you stand that racket?"

Tom gritted his teeth. "I guess you don't have an ear for music."

"Could be. I had a call from your counselor this afternoon. Do you know what she wants to talk to me about?"

"Didn't she tell you?"

"I didn't talk to her. Something came up."

"That figures," Tom said under his breath.

"I didn't hear that."

"Not to worry," Tom said.

"We'll go into this tomorrow. Sandy and I are going out for the evening."

"That figures," Tom said.

"See you."

As Bob left the room, Tom got up and turned the stereo on full-blast.

On the drive to the Stewarts', Bob said, "I had a call from Tom's guidance counselor this afternoon, but I didn't have time to talk to her. Do you have any idea what she wants?"

"Something about Tom's grades, I imagine," Sandy said. "She came into the store a day or so ago. Such a dowdy little thing. And no makeup."

"Did she say anything about Tom?"

"Yes."

"Well, why didn't you tell me?"

"Don't be so irritable! When have we seen one another to talk? We haven't had a meal together in days. You're always at that hospital."

"Let's not get into that again," Bob said wearily. "But you could have told me. We do live in the same house. Not the same bedroom, of course, but . . ."

"Let's not get into *that* again," Sandy echoed nervously. "I didn't mention the incident because you're so touchy about your son. You've always fostered the rivalry between Jimmy and Tom. And now that Jimmy's at Yale—"

"Oh, yes, your son, the student at Yale!"

"I don't think we should discuss this any further," Sandy said stiffly. And they rode in silence the rest of the way, both of them lost in thought.

The Stewarts were having a family party. Claire and Doug were there, along with the Stewart boys, Paul and Dan, and Dan's pretty blond girlfriend.

When Ellen opened the door, she said, "Hi! Where's Tom?"

Sandy said, "Oh, Ellen, you know boys that age!"

"I certainly do," Ellen answered. "When Paul and Dan were Tom's age, they thought anyone over twenty was senile. But I'm still sorry he didn't come."

"I didn't know he was invited," Bob said and was immediately sorry he had spoken. Ellen seemed not to hear, and Sandy ignored his comment

Somehow Bob got through the evening, hardly listening to the familiar sparring between Sandy and Claire. Neither liked the other, and Bob conceded that each woman had her reasons. Sandy didn't mention that Tom had been invited—that rankled. Doug worried him too. His color was terrible. Bob marveled that Claire didn't seem to notice. He looked at Sandy. How beautiful she was tonight! Even lovelier than when they'd met here all those years ago. He caught her eye, and she smiled. *Maybe tonight*, he thought.

As they were driving home, Bob said, "Why didn't you tell me that Ellen had invited Tom? And why didn't you tell Tom that he was invited?"

"Don't be tiresome," Sandy answered. "You know Tom. He wouldn't have gone. I saw no point in mentioning the invitation to him."

"I guess you're right at that," Bob said. They rode in silence for a bit, then Bob said, "In a way tonight reminded me of the night we met. Did you think of that?"

"No," Sandy answered.

"Paul and David were little boys then. One of them cried, and you rushed upstairs and talked to him. You were wonderful."

"So you wanted to marry me and buy a mother for Tom," Sandy said without emotion.

"You know that isn't true. I fell in love with you the moment I saw you."

"That's very romantic." After a pause, Sandy said, "Bob, I'm sorry I haven't been a better mother to Tom. I've tried. Honestly I have."

"I know," Bob said. "And I'm sorry I couldn't take the place of Jimmy's father."

"I believe you," Sandy said quietly. "Each boy needed more than we were able, or maybe willing, to give."

Bob drove into the garage and together they went upstairs. At the door to her room, Sandy stopped and opened the door. "Good night, Bob."

"Sleep well," Bob said and walked down the hall to his own room.

The next morning, Bob returned the counselor's call and arranged to meet her in her office that afternoon.

Mrs. Best came straight to the point. "Dr. Hughes, Tom is in deep trouble. He's failing one subject, and barely passing the others." She paused. "And he's using drugs."

What was she saying about Tom? Tom using drugs? He wanted to yell at her. She was so young, so smug, with her veneer of professionalism. What did she care about his kid? "Can't you—can't the school do something about this? Don't you people have any control?"

"Dr. Hughes, be reasonable. The school can't do everything. Parents have to do *their* part!"

"Where does he get drugs?"

"In many places. They're quite available. As a doctor, you must have seen . . ."

"But we're talking about my son. Tom." Bob looked at Mrs. Best. She looked as though she might cry. "I'm sorry, but this is devastating news. I'm not handling it too well. Can you advise me? What can I do?"

"You can talk to him—love him." She looked at Bob and tried to smile. "It's very hard, I know. There's one thing—Tom is very sensitive on the subject of his mother."

Bob nodded. "His mother and I have been divorced since Tom was two years old. Since then Tom hasn't seen her more than four times."

"I see," Mrs. Best said. "That must be very difficult for him. Tom will have to work that out for himself . . . if he can. But," she said briskly, "I wanted you to understand the situation. I'll continue to work with him. Maybe he should have outside help."

"Thank you," Bob said. "I'll think about it. And I'll try to try harder." He got to his feet, reached across the desk to shake her hand, and left the office. As he walked out of the building, feeling guilty and inadequate, he wondered where he'd be today if his own father had been as ineffective as *he* was. And not to notice that Tom was a user! He could spot an addict at twenty paces. Maybe he wasn't paying enough attention to Tom.

And why couldn't Tom have had a strong, loving mother like his own? Lisa! Headstrong, selfish, uncaring Lisa. Would she care if she knew? And why couldn't Sandy do more for Tom? She'd done well enough by Jimmy! But then the only thing Sandy cared about, other than Jimmy, was the store. She was a good businesswoman and she'd been successful. But she didn't have time for mothering. Come to think of it, he didn't have time for anything except doctoring!

He should take a little time off. He and Tom could go fishing. Fishing—that was the kind of thing men did with their sons. But thinking back, he didn't recall ever going fishing with his own father. Yet Dad was always there.

He was going to change. He'd be there for Tom. He'd show Tom he was concerned, that he really cared. He'd go back to the hospital and finish up the day's work and go home early. He'd take Tom out to dinner.

When Bob got home that night at seven, he found a note from Sandy. She planned to work until late at the store . . . there was a lot of ordering and work to do.

That was okay. He and Tom would go out to eat. He looked for Tom. He wasn't in his room. His car wasn't in the garage. Drat the boy! Didn't he even come home to eat? Where was he?

Chapter Nine

Sudden Death

Claire woke up as Doug came out of his dressing room. He was carrying his jacket and he seemed to be in a hurry. She sat up. "Good heavens! Are you just getting home or are you leaving?"

"I'm leaving, dear." Doug leaned over and kissed her.

"Wait! I'll make coffee. Fix you some breakfast." Claire was out of bed and putting on her robe.

"Go back to sleep. It's early," Doug said. "I'll get something at the hospital."

"Is there an emergency?"

"No. I can't sleep and there's a lot of work waiting for me at the office. Bye, darling. I'll call you later." And then he was out the door.

Claire hurried after him. When she opened the door into the hall, she saw the elevator door closing. What had gotten into Doug? If she didn't know him so well, she might think there was another woman. Claire smiled at the thought. But why was he working so hard? Only recently he'd stepped down as chief of surgery in favor of Bob Hughes. Now that Doug was director of Oakdale Memorial, he was working harder than ever. He really worried her. A little later, she'd call Ellen. Maybe David had said something.

Claire ate breakfast and spent a long time with the morning paper. But she was having trouble concentrating on the news. She felt restless, depressed.

Claire folded the paper and began to prowl through the apartment. The place was cozy and comfortable, but maybe they should think about buying a house. Doug had never had a real home of his own. Perhaps Doug would enjoy gardening. Roses could be fun. Anyway, it was time for a change. They were getting too stodgy, too set in routines. She'd discuss buying a house tonight at dinner. It might be a good idea for her to look at a few houses that were on the market. Then she'd know what she was talking about.

She called a realtor and made an appointment for that afternoon at two. Then she showered and dressed so she'd be ready to leave at the right time. She'd just finished putting on her makeup when she heard the buzzer. Who could that be? Maybe it was Ellen. That would be wonderful. They could have lunch.

Claire opened the door. "Ellen! And David! What a nice surprise!"

Ellen hugged her, and she could feel David's hand on her elbow. "What is this?" Claire asked. "It's so good to see you." She couldn't catch her breath. "Is something wrong?"

David drew her toward the sofa. "Sit here, Claire. I'm afraid we have bad news."

An ugly, nameless thing was all around her, strangling her, and she could hear someone moaning. "No, no, don't say it! It's Doug . . . Is it Doug? He's dead, isn't he?"

Ellen was holding her, rocking back and forth and

crooning, "Hush, Mama, hush. It's all right." Ellen hadn't called her "Mama" for years and years . . . That dark, blinding, deafening, numbing . . .

The next few weeks were a blur for Claire. The civilities of death, the funeral, the burying, the toleration of sympathy well meant, and the despairing anger. Ellen hardly left her side.

Then one morning, Claire woke up and lay staring at the ceiling, thinking of Doug. Dear, wonderful Doug, her best friend, her lover. She knew everything about his life, as though she had lived it with him. The orphanage where his history began was a part of her memory now. The awful poverty—she could smell it! His struggle made her ache, and then the elation of the realized goal of medical school.

His only love had been medicine, until Claire. And why was she hiding like a wounded animal? She couldn't go on hiding. She must stop! Claire got out of bed, calling, "Ellen!"

Ellen came into the room. "Good morning, Mother. I've been waiting for you."

Claire grabbed her robe and headed for the bathroom. "I'm well and I'm going on with my life. I want you to go home and tend to your family. Thank you for everything. You're a wonderful daughter and now I want to be alone." When Ellen didn't move, Claire said, "I mean it. Go home! By the way, I'm taking you to lunch at the country club. See if your friend Sandy will join us." She stormed into the bathroom and slammed the door.

Ellen hesitated. When she heard the shower turned on full force, she went to the telephone and dialed Sandy's office.

At first, Sandy said, "Oh, Ellen, I really shouldn't. There's so much to do today."

"Please, Sandy, this is the first indication that Mother may be coming back to the land of the living."

"In that case," Sandy said, "see you at one!"

Claire felt physically weak, like someone who'd survived a long illness. On the other hand, she felt rather proud of herself. She was coping. She'd called the maitre d' at the club and arranged the luncheon. She'd dressed and had her hair done. Ready to entertain, she asked to be seated at the table in order to be on hand to greet her guests. She wondered what had possessed her to ask Sandy. She didn't particularly enjoy her company. Then she realized that she'd invited Sandy to give Ellen a brief respite from herself. She settled back in her chair, deciding that Sandy wasn't all bad.

Evidently Sandy and Ellen had met in the parking lot. At any rate, they were walking toward her and smiling. Claire reached out to both of them. To her surprise, she was genuinely glad to see Sandy.

"How lovely you look, Mrs. Cassen," Sandy said as she sat down.

"Doesn't she!" Ellen said.

"That's nice," Claire said. "It's been a long time since I noticed. As you grow older, the joy in your image—in your looks—lessens."

"But you're not old," Sandy said.

Claire patted her hand. "You had to say that. But now that the subject has come up, I'm feeling very old."

"Mother! You're only sixty-two."

"Only!" Claire gave her throaty laugh and nodded at the handsome young man at the bar who raised his glass to her. "Who's that?"

Sandy glanced across the room. "Michael Shea."

"He was a protege of Doug's," Ellen said.

"Oh, yes, I remember now—Doug brought him to dinner once. I thought he looked familiar."

"He's very familiar." Sandy told her, laughing.

"What does that mean?" Claire asked.

"Nothing, really," Sandy said.

"He's quite attractive and he's single," Ellen pointed out. "I suppose it's only natural that there would be gossip."

"If he were married, there'd be more," Claire said. "But what is a doctor doing at the club for lunch? No doctor I know lunches here during the week!"

"That's Michael," Sandy murmured.

"Boys will be boys, I suppose," Claire said. "I have something to say. I apologize for the way I've been carrying on. I hate public displays of any kind." She put her hand on Ellen's. "I'm sorry, darling. From now on I'm going private."

"Oh, Mrs. Cassen! I think you've been very brave. Bob's mother thinks you're remarkable."

Claire smiled at Sandy. "That's kind of you and Nancy, but I haven't been brave at all. I've been a complete mess. I guess it was the shock—"

"You didn't know?" Sandy said in surprise. "I thought you knew about Doug's heart. David said . . ."

Sandy grew quiet when she felt the pressure of Ellen's foot.

"What did David say?" Claire's tone was icy.

"Mother." Ellen paused. "Mother, David and Bob knew that Doug had an inoperable heart condition. But he, that is, Doug didn't want you to worry."

"Doug kept something from me! I don't believe it. We shared everything!"

Ellen was almost crying. "Mother, Doug wanted you to be happy. He didn't want you to be afraid—"

"Doug didn't trust me! Is that what you're saying?"

"Oh, Mother, please—"

"So Doug had a secret and all of you were in on it!" Her voice rose. "Let's not let Claire know. Let's keep everything from Claire!"

"Mother, everyone can hear you."

"I don't care! You've been treating me like a child. I'll act like a child." Claire looked into Ellen's eyes. "Oh, honey, why didn't someone say something to prepare me?" Claire pushed back her chair and stood. "Enjoy your lunch, ladies. I'm leaving." She walked briskly across the dining room and disappeared from view.

Ellen ran after her, but Claire was gone. Sandy caught up with Ellen, and they hurried toward the parking lot.

"Oh, Ellen, I feel terrible. I wish I hadn't said that, but I thought she knew."

"She was bound to find out sometime. I wish I'd told her long ago myself!"

"There she goes!" Sandy pointed to Claire's brown sedan, speeding through the exit gate.

Ellen groaned. "Did you see that? She didn't stop at the sign. She's going to hurt herself."

"Where do you suppose she's going?" Sandy asked.

"I can't imagine. You go back to work, Sandy. I'm going to Mother's apartment. Maybe she's going home."

"Call me," Sandy said and moved off to her own car.

Claire was furious and glad of it. Rage was much headier than grief. Doug! Damn him! The ultimate put-down! He'd trusted her with everything but the truth. But he'd told everyone else. Even that frigid bitch Sandy knew! Did he know he was dying when he left so early that morning? Creeping off to die at his desk? Of course he knew! Claire heard a siren and jammed on the brakes. Now what! The police car whizzed by. She couldn't even get arrested!

The engine was dead! "Hell!" Claire stamped on the starter and stepped on the gas. The motor whined, but didn't catch. "Flooded! What next?"

Claire got out of the car, leaving the door partially open, and stomped off down the street. She flagged a cab, and climbed in. "Take me to the nearest car dealer," she told the driver.

Soon the cab stopped, and the driver turned to look at Claire. "How's this one, lady?"

"It's lovely. Thank you so much." Claire gave the driver a twenty, saying, "Do keep the change," and swept into the showroom.

A red Porsche gleamed under spotlights. Claire opened the door on the driver's side and got in.

At once a salesman was peering at her through the open window. "She's a beauty, isn't she!"

"Absolutely gorgeous," Claire said.

"I have other makes and models to show you," the salesman said. "For instance, there's that blue Mercedes, the four-door job over there."

"Oh, but I like this one," Claire purred. "I'll take it!"

"This'll make a great birthday gift for some young fella. Your son?"

"I don't have a son. Now do the things you have to do, and I'll take this with me. Fill in the numbers on the check and I'll sign."

The salesman stared at the check Claire had given him. "Yes, ma'am. You know, it generally takes a few days to get the papers in order and all that."

"Surely you can do something to speed the process. I need this car desperately." She smiled a dazzling smile.

The salesman looked at the check, then at Claire. "I'll try, ma'am. I sure will try."

After an hour's wait and a brandy provided by the dealer himself, Claire had her sports car. The salesman tried to give her a few instructions, but she waved him aside, got into her car, and roared away down the boulevard.

The salesman watched until the car was out of sight. "There goes one crazy lady."

The dealer slapped him on the shoulder. "I wish there were dozens like her. Good day's work, Peavy!"

"Thank you, sir." He was going to get a fat commission, but he felt a little guilty. She was kind of a nice old girl, but she wasn't up to driving that car. Didn't have the reflexes.

By four that afternoon, Claire was back at the beauty salon, demanding to see the manager.

"Is something wrong, Mrs. Cassen?" he asked.

"Indeed there is. I'm so mousy-colored. Charles, I want you to dye my hair!"

"We never say 'dye,' Mrs. Cassen. What tint do you have in mind?"

"Don't pout, Charles. I want to be blond. Utterly, supremely blond."

Charles glanced at the receptionist and back at Claire. "Why don't you come back tomorrow and we'll discuss it then? It's getting near closing time."

"You're hedging, Charles. If you won't turn me into a blonde, I'll find someone who will."

"All right, Mrs. Cassen. But if you don't like it . . ."

Claire loved it. She left the salon a little before seven with hair the color of honey. But when she was outside and walking along the dark street toward her car, she felt lonely and a little sad. She drove slowly all the way home. She was terribly tired, so tired she could barely see the street, and was almost blinded by the lights. As she entered the lobby of the apartment house, the elevators seemed too far away. Somehow she was at her door turning the key in the lock and pushing the door open. And there was Ellen.

Ellen grabbed her, and it was a good thing. She might have fallen. "Mother! Are you all right? I've been so worried." Ellen gasped and took a step backward. "Mother! Your hair! What have you done?"

"Do you like it? You know, darling, I'm very tired. If you don't mind being alone, I think I'll go straight to bed."

Claire went to her room and fell across the bed. Ellen undressed her and helped her under the covers. Then she went into the living room to call David, telling him briefly what had happened. "I think I'd better stay here again tonight," she said.

"I think so too," David said. "But you mustn't worry. Your mother's going to be fine. Right now she's still in shock."

"I know. But this morning she seemed her old self again . . . almost."

"It's to be expected. Grief is an illness."

Ellen went back into Claire's room to sit beside the bed. The hair color was rather nice, she thought. But it made her look different, not much like her mother or the boys' grandmother.

Claire slept until eleven the next morning. Ellen had become so worried that she called David. He said, "Sleep is what she needs. Don't worry."

But Ellen worried in spite of what David said. She had been awakened much earlier by a policeman at the door, inquiring about Claire's "abandoned vehicle." Ellen hadn't known what he was talking about, but she'd agreed to pay the towing charges.

When Claire did wake up, she seemed her old self again and Ellen was relieved. David was correct in his judgment. She could understand that her mother was going through a painful recovery.

Over her coffee, Claire said, "You were so good to worry about me, darling. But I'm fine. Now you run along. I don't want to take up any more of your day." She was relieved when Ellen finally left. What had Ellen done to get her so angry yesterday? Never mind! Whatever it was, it was unimportant. She didn't mention the new car because she didn't think of it until Ellen was going out the door. There'd be plenty of time to tell her later.

Claire dressed with care. She thought she'd do a little shopping. She didn't like a thing that was hanging in her closet. All her dresses were so dowdy and matronly. Doug had never paid any attention to what she'd worn. He'd said, "You look very nice." Nice! She was fed up with looking nice!

As Claire was leaving the apartment, her phone rang. "Drat!" Who could that be? She picked up the phone and heard a tentative, "Claire?"

"Nancy! How are you? How good to hear your voice!"

"How are you, Claire? Chris and I haven't seen you since— Could you come to dinner tonight?"

"Tonight? Let me think . . ." She wasn't in the mood for Nancy and Chris. They were so good and she'd known them so long. Should she lie? "Nancy, I can't think as far ahead as tonight. I'm on my way out the door to go shopping."

"I see, then maybe . . ."

Nancy sounded hurt. Damn! "Nancy, I'll be by for you in twenty minutes. We'll have lunch and you'll go shopping with me."

Nancy stammered and faltered, but finally agreed. Claire was pleased. What fun it would be to watch

Nancy's expression when she saw the sports car and the new hair. She was so eager to see Nancy's reactions, she drove faster than she should have all the way to the Hughes'.

Nancy's reaction was even more amusing than Claire had imagined. For five minutes, all she could do was sputter and fume. "Claire, I don't know what you're thinking of. This car! Well, my goodness! It looks dangerous. Do you think it's the thing for you?"

For a time Claire was afraid she wouldn't persuade Nancy to ride with her. When Nancy finally lowered herself into the car, she sat with her back braced against the bucket seat, grasping the handle with both hands.

Claire watched her for a minute or two and said, "Nancy, you're so funny. Relax!"

Nancy kept her eyes on the road and didn't speak.

While they were having lunch, Claire told Nancy all about the way Doug had kept the truth from her. Nancy was surprised. She'd never heard a thing about Doug's heart condition, so she'd been shocked, as well as grieved, by his death. Claire didn't know whether to believe her or not.

Claire had put Doug out of her mind by the time she and Nancy arrived at Chez Elle, the boutique on the fifth floor of Mayer's Department Store. She told the clerk, "I must refurbish my wardrobe." And she paid no attention when Nancy said, "Why, Claire, you have beautiful clothes. And so many!"

The clerk studied Claire through narrowed eyes. "You're an eight, I believe." She left and quickly returned with several dresses.

Claire smiled and shook her head. "They're nice, but not what I had in mind. I'd like something with a little more zing."

The clerk smiled. "I believe I know what you mean."

She disappeared into another room.

Claire turned to Nancy. "I've been waiting for you to comment on my hair. What do you think?"

Nancy took a deep breath. "Well, Claire, I hardly know what to think. It makes you look so different. A little . . ." She looked at Claire, unable to continue.

"You don't like it! That's all right, Nancy. I like it! It makes me feel . . ." She searched for the word. "I don't know, I just feel . . . lighter on my feet. Does that make sense?"

"Yes, Claire, it does make sense. It's wonderful to see you happy again."

The clerk returned with a greater variety of clothing.

"That's more like it!" Claire said. "I'll try the sequin, the white crepe." She smiled. "I'll try them all!"

"I'll wait here," Nancy said. Something was troubling Claire. She wasn't herself. Nancy wondered if Ellen had noticed anything odd about the way Claire was behaving. Then Nancy gasped. Claire was sauntering out of the dressing room wearing the jade sequin dress. My, it did fit her very well. It was street-length, perhaps a bit too short. But it just wasn't Claire. Claire had never worn that type of dress, not even when she was in her twenties. She could sense Claire watching her.

"What do you think?"

"I don't know, Claire. It's . . . colorful."

Claire whirled, watching herself in the mirror. "I like the play of the skirt, don't you?"

"Well, yes, I do. But is it comfortable? It seems just a little tight through the bust."

"Feels great." She looked at the clerk. "What do you think? Do you think it fits?"

"Oh, perfectly. Madam has such a lovely, youthful figure."

"Mmm." Claire kept her eyes on the mirror. "But do you think it's me?"

Nancy cleared her throat. "Well now, Claire. Quite frankly, I don't."

Claire lifted her head. "Well, it's the me I want to be! I'll take it!"

Nancy got to her feet. "Claire, you're going to be busy for quite a while trying on other things. I think I'd better leave now. I'll drop by the office and get a ride home with Chris. Come see us when you can."

"Yes, I will," Claire said, hardly aware that Nancy was leaving. She was dying to try on the platinum wool suit with the fox collar.

Chapter Ten
Foolish Heart

Within the next few months, Claire made a number of changes in her life. She bought a house on Country Club Lane, near Sandy and Bob's estate, and hired a decorator from Chicago. When Ellen heard about the house, she said, "Oh, Mother, do you think you should live in a house alone?"

"Why not?" Claire said. "It's only a little house."

"It's lovely, but it's so secluded and so cut off from any other house. Are you sure you won't be lonely?"

"I'll give parties. I've met a number of new people." Claire suspected she'd be lonely wherever she lived.

Finally everything had been done on the house, and Claire had time on her hands. She began to spend more time at the Oakdale Country Club. Tonight she was in her accustomed place at the end of the bar, where she could see friends coming into the room. She had just finished her first Scotch and was trying to catch the bartender's eye to order her second.

He looked her way. "What'll it be, Mrs. Cassen?"

"The same. No, make it a double." Claire looked

around the dimly lit room. "Where is everyone, Hank?"

"It's early yet, Mrs. Cassen. Don't you worry. They'll be here." He put her drink on the bar in front of her.

Claire lit a cigarette and inhaled. She'd taken up smoking again. She'd smoked when she was a kid, but gave it up before Ellen was born and never went back to it. Doug would have a fit if he knew she was smoking again. She picked up her glass and took a sip, trying not to make a face. She hated Scotch. Why had she ordered a double? She looked into the mirror, but could see only her own reflection. The room was so dark. It must be nearly six, almost time for Michael to get here. She smiled, thinking of Michael. Even though he always made it clear how much he'd admired Doug, he was a very different kind of doctor. He didn't spend all his time at the hospital. Claire wished he'd hurry. He was fun to talk with. She felt a tap on her shoulder and turned. "Young Shea! I thought you'd never get here!"

Michael kissed her cheek. "It's early, Lady Fair. But here I am ready to do your bidding."

Claire sighed happily. "Then sit, youngster, and tell me about your day."

"Let's talk about yours." Michael picked up her drink and sniffed. "How many have you had?"

"This is my second. Will you have dinner with me?"

"Maybe. If you'll ply me with liquor first." He snapped his fingers and when Jimmy looked his way, Michael said, "Ginger ale."

"You don't drink—do you, Michael?" Claire said.

"Not much. I need a clear head and a steady hand at all times."

Claire didn't comment. Sometimes Michael made

her feel ill-at-ease, as though he were studying her. But she was being ridiculous.

Michael put his hand on hers. "You're quiet tonight. Is something the matter?"

Although Claire liked to have him touch her, she withdrew her hand. Someone might notice Michael's innocent gesture and misunderstand. She shivered. "No. Nothing's the matter. But this has been such a long, cold, rainy, dreary day."

"I know," Michael said quietly, looking into her eyes.

Claire turned her head. She wished Michael wouldn't look at her that way. She was almost old enough to be his mother. Who was she kidding? Michael was thirty-six, the same age as Sandy. She was old enough to be his mother, all right!

"You're a loner, aren't you, Claire?"

"Of course not!"

"Don't be angry. I'm a loner too and I don't particularly like it. A bar's no place for us. We should be in our own home, sitting by our own hearth."

"What a cozy picture!" Claire laughed nervously.

Michael looked hurt. "Why do you always make fun of me, Claire?"

Claire couldn't think of an answer. Michael was right—she did talk down to him.

"I'm no different from other people, Claire. Maybe you don't believe this, but I get lonely. I'm here because I don't want to go back to my empty apartment."

Michael lonely! The idea seemed preposterous to Claire. "You don't need to be lonely. A handsome, intelligent, charming young man like you." She could feel him watching her. He reminded her of a big cat, a leopard maybe, with muscles coiled and ready to spring. "Have you ever been married?"

"No! It hasn't been one of my priorities."

"Well, maybe you should get married." She was trying for a motherly tone. "You must find a nice girl—there must be literally dozens after you, settle down, have babies."

"No children! That's one reason I've never married. All the women I've ever known have wanted children!"

Claire emptied her glass and set it down. "You will, Michael. Someday you'll want a child of your own. A son maybe with your copper-colored hair and big blue eyes." Mercy! She was getting carried away. She'd better have another drink. She nodded at Hank. "Now that I think of it, I've seen you with a very pretty blond girl several times."

"What blonde?" Michael asked gruffly.

"Heavens, I don't know her name. I saw you dancing with her one night." Claire remembered the incident very well. What a lovely couple they made, and how it hurt her to see them together.

"You're the only blonde I care to know," Michael said and reached for her hand. "This is no place to talk. Let's get out of here." He started for the door, pulling her after him.

Claire was giggling. "Stop it, Michael. Wait! Hank," she called, "put everything on my tab."

Michael stopped at the coat check. "Mrs. Cassen's wrap. The platinum mink—that's the one." He helped Claire into her coat and fastened the clasp at the neck, whispering, "All set?"

Claire felt like a little girl, loved, adored, protected. Dreamily she watched Michael talking with the doorman. He turned to her. "Would you rather take your car?"

"If you'll drive."

"Of course." He nodded to the attendant. "The red Porsche."

When they were in the car, Claire leaned back and closed her eyes. The drinks had made her sleepy. "Where are we going?"

"Do you care?"

"Not much." The air was much colder. Although the rain had stopped, the sky was overcast. "It feels like snow," Claire said.

"You want to talk about the weather?"

Claire turned her head so she could watch Michael's face, see his changing expressions. She loved the way his hair curled on his neck. It wasn't easy to see him in the dim light from the dashboard, and perhaps that was just as well. He was much too good-looking, and she was much too old to be noticing.

Michael broke the silence. "I love this car, Claire. It makes no demands. It performs. A perfect machine!"

"It suits you," Claire said. "I haven't the faintest idea why I bought it."

"Well, why did you?"

"I don't know," Claire answered. "I was a little crazy the day I got it. I've done a lot of crazy things lately."

"I'd like to be crazy the way you are, Claire. But it takes a hell of a lot of money or a good credit line."

Claire smiled. "Do you think money would make you happy?"

"Stupid question!" He glanced at Claire. "How rich are you? Do you even know?"

"Now you're being a brat again," Claire answered. "Of course I know. Why are we talking like this? And where are we going?"

"Calm down, Lady Fair. I know a wonderful little inn. It isn't far. We'll have dinner. Okay?"

"Okay."

Michael kept his eyes on the road. "For a minute there, you were treating me like an adult."

"Don't I always?"

"Never. In fact, you work so hard at treating me like a child that I . . ."

"That you what?"

"Well, I wonder. That's all."

"I'm sorry, Michael. But I can hardly treat you like a peer. After all, there's a great difference in our ages."

"Eighteen years."

"Well, there you are," Claire said, too vain to correct his mistake.

"Lots of women marry men eighteen years older than they are. No one thinks anything of that."

"I do," Claire said firmly. "I think they're marrying for money. But who's talking about marriage?"

"We are!" The car slowed. "This is the place," Michael said. "McGinty's Tavern. You're going to love this, Claire." Michael parked the car next to a large frame house. Neon beer signs, blinking in the windows, were the only signs of human habitation.

"I've never heard of this place." Claire folded her arms, refusing to move.

Michael reached across and opened the door on Claire's side. "Come on. Don't let the neons scare you. This place is perfectly respectable and the food's great."

"It had better be," Claire grumbled as she climbed out of the car. She balked again before they reached the entrance. "This really looks like a dive."

Michael leered at her and opened the door. "It takes an old-timer like you to recognize a white-slaver when she sees one."

Shaking with laughter, Claire went inside. A large fair-haired man wearing a tuxedo blocked their way, but after a brief exchange with Michael, the man led them to an alcove in a dining room paneled in dark wood. Claire noticed that only a few tables were occupied. She stumbled and almost fell against a table, cursing herself for not wearing her glasses.

"Over here," Michael said. He helped her off with her coat and seated her at the table. A waiter brought drinks and disappeared into the gloom.

"Alone at last," Michael said. "Now we can talk. You know quite a bit about me. I want to know all about you."

"There's nothing of interest to tell." This creepy place was getting to Claire. Michael seemed a little strange too. If she were twenty years younger, she might think Michael was making a pass.

"You're shivering," Michael said. "Drink up!" He waited while she tasted her drink. "That's good. Now let's begin at the beginning. Where were you born?"

Claire groaned. "You're very sweet to try and draw me out, Michael. But it's a dull, dull story." She sipped her drink. "Not bad. I wonder if I'm developing a taste for Scotch."

Michael grasped her wrist. "Claire, talk to me. Where were you born?" He applied more pressure.

"Stop that! You're hurting me," Claire said. "I'll tell you anything you care to know." She smiled as Michael settled back in his chair. "I was born south of here and it's none of your business when. My father died before I was born, and I was an orphan by the time I was three. So I went to live with my grandfather. He died when I was seven and after that I lived with one relative and then with another. I wasn't very happy." Michael moved his chair closer to hers and put his arm around her. "What are you doing?" Claire sounded irritable.

"I'm showing my sympathy."

"Never mind. I don't want it," she said, drawing away.

"Sorry," Michael said. "Go on."

"When I was seventeen, I went to the state university. There I met Jim Lowell. We fell in love and we got married. Jim's father, Judge Lowell, was my guardian, and that was a problem."

"And what was wrong with that?" Michael asked.

"Judge Lowell was afraid that people would think he'd arranged the marriage so that Jim could get at my money."

Michael's arm was around her again. "And did he?"

"Of course not. Jim didn't need my money. In fact, he didn't need anything I had, at least not for long. Jim had a short attention span."

"But you had Ellen."

"Thank God for Ellen," Claire said. "Then Jim died and I married Doug and Doug died . . . and that's the end of my story."

"And you've been acting like it's the end of your life." Michael sat back, watching her. "Just how rich are you?"

Claire laughed uneasily. "Michael, you're impossible. What do you care? Do you think I'm going to adopt you?"

"Oh, no. I expect you to marry me."

"You can't be serious."

"But I am. You're everything I want in a woman. You're rich, good company, and sexy."

Claire gulped the rest of her drink and put the empty glass on the table. "Now I've heard it all. Why do you think I'd marry you?"

"Because I'm good-looking, sexy, and young. What more could you want?"

Claire began putting on her coat. "I'd better go home.

Will you drive me back to Oakdale?"

"Wait," Michael said. He took her in his arms and kissed her.

At first she was startled. Then she could feel herself responding and pulled away. "Really, I must go."

"No, Claire. We can stay here tonight."

"So that's what you were saying to that thug! You were renting a room." She picked up her purse and stalked toward the door. "I'm leaving. You can stay here or come with me, as you like."

Michael held up her car keys. "Look, Claire, you can't go."

At the door, Claire turned. "I carry a spare set."

Michael followed her outside and held the car door for her. He got in on the driver's side and started the motor. When he turned on the headlights, they could see a mist of fine snow. "I don't think we can make it back to Oakdale. We'd better stay here," Michael said.

"Would you like me to drive?" Claire asked.

"Never!" He backed the car out and headed out of the parking lot to the highway and toward Oakdale. "I'm disappointed in you, Claire. I was hoping you'd compromise me and we'd have to get married."

"I'd rather not talk about this anymore."

"All right, my dear. But I promise you we'll discuss this again."

Michael drove her home and asked to spend the night. When she told him he couldn't stay, he said he wouldn't leave until she'd shown him through her new house. An hour and a half later, Claire was dialing for a cab when Michael said he couldn't leave. The snow was six inches deep, and a cab couldn't get through.

"Michael, I give up," Claire said. "You can sleep in the guest room."

Claire went to bed, but couldn't sleep. Thinking

about Michael made her restless. His voice, his touch, the way he'd kissed her. She knew he couldn't find her attractive, but there was passion in his kiss. How could he possibly feel anything for her? He was pretending! Her aging flesh must repel him. No, it was unthinkable. He was teasing her, laughing at her. What a mean thing for him to do! She must get to sleep now or she'd look terrible in the morning.

A little later, Claire didn't know how long she'd been asleep, but Michael's arms were around her. Then his hand was caressing her body. She turned toward him, and his mouth was on hers and she forgot there had ever been a yesterday. She was young and alive and desirable and she could sense how desperately Michael wanted her.

Claire woke with the sunlight streaming through the window, searing her eyelids. She could smell coffee brewing and she felt happy. Why was she happy? Before she could remember, Michael came through the open bedroom door, carrying a tray. She must look terrible in daylight, she thought, longing to hide from him.

Michael was smiling. "Good morning. You were wonderful! I must run now—I'm late. Call you later. Enjoy your breakfast."

Claire heard a car coming slowly up the drive. "Is that your cab?"

"I don't think so." Michael parted the curtains. "It's Ellen."

Claire got out of bed to look. The view was breathtaking. Heavy, unbroken snow covered the yard, plantings and driveway, everything except the tire tracks of Ellen's jeep. Ellen could see that she was Claire's first visitor for the day.

"Oh, good heavens," Claire moaned. "Hide! Do

something! Ellen mustn't see you!"

"Don't be prudish." Michael was enjoying the situation. "We'll tell Ellen we're engaged."

"Engaged! Oh, Michael, please hide. Ellen will be in the house in a minute. She has a key."

The front door opened, and Ellen called, "Mother, are you all right?"

"In here," Claire said weakly.

Claire covered her face. Ellen was coming down the hall now. Michael didn't have time to hide if he wanted.

"I was worried about you," Ellen was saying. "I didn't want you to be snowed in and all alone." Ellen was in the doorway, looking at Michael. "Oh! Dr. Shea."

"Good morning, Ellen. I'm just leaving. Nice to see you."

Ellen flushed. "Good morning, uh . . . Michael. I'm glad you're all right, Mother. I'll just run along."

Before Claire could think of something to say, Ellen was gone. "Oh, Michael, what am I going to do with you?"

"I think you're going to marry me. My cab's here. Goodbye for now, love. I'll call you later," he said as he left.

Claire listened to the cab drive away. It was too soon to reach Ellen. What could she say to her? She had to talk to someone. Nancy? Good lord, no! What should she do? Ellen would think she'd lost her mind. Should she marry Michael? Unthinkable! But the idea did have a certain appeal. She'd give it some thought.

Claire was not the only one with mixed emotions. All the way to the hospital Michael was wondering what he was getting himself into. The idea of marrying

Claire had been in the back of his mind for some time. Actually, he'd been thinking about it since the day he saw Claire at lunch at the club soon after Doug's death.

Michael knew he had a promising future, but the future seemed a long time away. He was on the staff at Memorial and was just starting a private practice, but that took time. Meanwhile he was having serious cash-flow problems.

And there was Claire. He'd always found her to be an interesting "older" woman, smart-looking, well-groomed, poised. She could do a lot for him. If he could arrange five years of financial security, he could make it big!

But then things had never been easy. He was an only child with a beautiful, demanding, widowed mother. His father had been an only child too, the son who was expected to rebuild the family fortune. The challenge had been too great, and Michael's father became a helpless drunk. Michael had been humiliated, growing up in the biggest, shabbiest house in his hometown. He'd had to wait to go to college. He'd driven a coal truck for three years, saving his money. Then he'd gone to a small, exclusive men's school on a scholarship. He'd been a freshman at twenty! God! How he'd hated everything about it. Now he had a chance to make up for the slights, the shirts with the turned collars, for all the things he'd done without. And Claire wasn't so bad. Then if things got dull around Claire's gem of a house, there was Lorraine!

Lorraine! She was soft where Claire was angular. She was dewy and fresh and very satisfactory. Lorraine, the dancer. She might be furious at first, knowing he'd married Claire, but she'd understand. She was pretty damn hungry too. What she'd give to get away from that sleazy club she worked in! And maybe he could help . . . after he married Claire and financial arrangements were made. Lorraine had always wanted to study ballet. Now maybe she could. He'd manage something. Maybe even a fox jacket. Lorraine loved showy things.

And Claire was level-headed. She'd go for a prenuptial contract. Too bad he had to make rounds this morning. He'd love a nap. Making love could be work!

After the shock wore off, Ellen became frightened. She had to talk to her mother, get her off this kick with Dr. Shea. But when she tried to talk to Claire, she wouldn't listen. She didn't want to talk at all.

Ellen said, "Mother . . . Michael Shea! There must be someone more suitable, someone nearer your own age. I know you're lonely, and I understand that, but Mother . . ."

Claire didn't hear her, not even for a minute. Ellen knew there was nothing she could do.

Around ten that morning, David called Ellen. He could sense that something was bothering her and finally persuaded her to tell him. He was worried when he put down the phone. Ellen was correct in thinking that Claire might marry Shea. And David was pretty sure that Shea had marriage on his mind. On the other hand, this could blow over, and it was better not to discuss it.

But everyone on the staff at Memorial knew that Dr. Shea was after Dr. Cassen's widow. One of the nurses, a former girlfriend of Michael's, had seen the pair at McGinty's and had overheard most of their conversation. She'd also watched Michael's routine and found it familiar.

Bob heard something about the incident, but wrote

it off as gossip and almost forgot the story. Sandy heard a customer talking about the affair early in the afternoon and believed every word she heard.

While Nancy was getting her hair done that afternoon, she heard one of the operators talking about Mrs. Cassen and Dr. Shea. She didn't want to make a fuss, so she kept still. But as soon as she got home, she called Claire. "I know this is none of my business, Claire, but I really think that something should be done to stop this ridiculous story."

"You're quite right, Nancy," Claire said.

"Just tell me what to do. I don't want to say a thing to make the gossip worse than it is."

"You misunderstand me, Nancy. I meant you're right that it's none of your business."

Nancy took a deep breath. "I see. I'm sorry to have bothered you, Claire."

"That's quite all right. How's Chris?"

The conversation continued along familiar lines. Nancy was hurt, but she wasn't going to let Claire know that she was. In time, Claire would be her old self again. And certainly their friendship was strong enough to withstand a few barbs from Claire.

Claire felt uneasy after talking to Nancy and she wished Michael would call. As the day wore on and he didn't, she was feeling less secure about herself and about Michael. *I'm acting like a teenager*, she told herself. *Waiting for the phone to ring is insanity. I'll get out of here.* She made an appointment at the beauty salon and left, thinking it infinitely better not to know that Michael wasn't calling.

Claire drove slowly and carefully. The streets hadn't been fully cleared of last night's snow. She passed a parked car that looked familiar. Of course! Michael's car and he was in it! She was going to stop until she noticed he wasn't alone. His head was turned away from her, and he was talking to a blond girl who appeared to be crying. Claire jammed her foot on the accelerator. Damn him! Maybe he hadn't seen her! But how could he miss her silly car!

Claire drove home, put a few things in a traveling case and called a cab to drive her to the airport. She'd get on the first plane leaving Oakdale, regardless of the destination. She was a silly old fool.

An hour later, Claire boarded a jet for Chicago. She hadn't the least idea where she'd go from there. Now that she was on her way she felt almost peaceful, as though all her troubles were twenty-thousand feet below her on the ground. She didn't see one familiar face on the plane, and that was a relief. She was away from the restrictions of being Claire Lowell Cassen.

At O'Hare she got on a plane for New York. By now she was making plans. There should be a nine o'clock flight for Paris. Paris would be a relief. She wouldn't know a soul and she couldn't speak the language. So she'd be entirely alone and that would be wonderful.

One week later, Claire was enjoying a drink in the Ritz bar. She'd spent the afternoon shopping in charming little boutiques along the Rue de Rivoli. Her packages were on the seat beside her—she hadn't bothered to take them upstairs yet—and she was deciding whether or not to go to the opera. The thought of Michael crossed her mind and she smiled. How silly she'd been. Such a fuss. She'd enjoyed the night with Michael, and why not? There was nothing so unusual in an older woman and a younger man. In Paris one saw that sort of thing quite often.

She felt a hand on her shoulder. Startled, she looked up into Michael's smiling face.

"Move over." Michael slid in beside her and covered her hand with his. "I got here as fast as I could, Lady Fair, but it took awhile to find you."

"But why are you here? I can't believe it. How did you know where I was?"

"I'm here because we're getting married. We'll have a lovely honeymoon. How thoughtful of you to hide in Paris!"

"But how did you find me? Did Ellen tell you where I was?"

"I didn't ask," he said with dignity. He wasn't going to tell Claire, but he'd hired a detective to trace her to Paris, reasoning that it was a sound investment. "And now that we're together again we must make plans."

This is happening too fast, Claire thought. There were questions she should ask, but what were they? Oh, yes. Now she remembered. "But, Michael, what about that girl?"

Michael looked blank. "What girl?"

"I saw you with her. You were in your car and she was crying. You know who I mean. The blonde!"

Michael looked at the ceiling, as though trying to remember. "Oh," he said, "now I remember. The poor girl whose brother just died." (Actually, she was crying because she'd learned she was pregnant.)

Claire frowned. "Of course I didn't know what she was crying about."

"Claire dear, you know very well that doctors have patients. You've had enough experience to know that you can't be suspicious and suspect every woman your husband sees professionally."

Michael was right. How could she be so silly? And Paris was a lovely place for a honeymoon. Tomorrow they'd go shopping. They'd get a suit for Michael to wear to the wedding. And as soon as they got back to

Oakdale, after the honeymoon, they'd get together with Chris Hughes and set up a financial arrangement for Michael.

She smiled. "Michael, wait till you see my room. It's lovely."

Chapter Eleven
A Beginning . . .

As it turned out, Claire and Michael didn't get married in Paris, after all. Michael decided legal matters were much too complicated in France. There was an eight-day wait, as well as other tedious technicalities. So they spent a stimulating two-week honeymoon in Paris and flew back to Chicago to get married.

Ellen and David had no idea of what was going on and couldn't have done anything about it if they had known. After many discussions, they decided to accept and support any decision Claire might make.

It was hard, though, because Ellen knew that Michael was certainly wrong for her mother. David saw her concern and suggested that they give a party, a little reception for the newlyweds.

"Do you think we should?"

"Absolutely. We'll give a little reception for their closest friends."

Ellen perked up after that. The idea appealed to her. "I guess I'll check with Mother the minute she gets home."

Claire and Michael returned to Oakdale the next day. While Michael was in his apartment, packing his things to move into his new house, Claire stopped by to see Ellen.

Ellen saw Claire getting out of a shiny blue sedan and ran out to greet her. They hugged each other for a moment and then went into the house hand in hand.

"Now that the tears and cheers are over, tell me what's been going on in Oakdale while I was away." Claire slipped out of her coat and let it drop to the floor.

Ellen picked it up and hung it in the closet. "Umm, nice dress."

Claire smoothed the red fabric over her hips. "This old thing? I got it in Paris."

"You're driving a different car," Ellen said.

"Yes, I got it in Oakdale. It's more my speed, I think. Michael adores the red one, and now it's his."

"Good!" Ellen said emphatically. "You scared me, driving that thing. Come on, let's have a cup of coffee."

Claire followed Ellen into the kitchen. "How are the boys?"

"Fine. Dan's dating a fellow-resident at Memorial."

"A girl, I hope," Claire said.

Ellen smiled. "The feminists will hate you! Her name's Susan Burke."

"How about Paul? Does he have a girl?"

"I'm afraid he likes Susan, too. The boys worry me, the way they invariably like the same girl." Ellen shook her head. "By the way, David and I would like to give a party for you and Michael."

Claire frowned. "Do you think it's a good idea?"

"Yes! Unless, for some reason you don't think . . ."

Claire squared her shoulders. "By all means, give us

a party. We'll love it!"

"Good!" Ellen was relieved. "Now whom shall we ask?"

"Don't make it a big party. Just our closest, oldest friends, I think. The boys . . . Oh, you know who to ask," Claire said.

"What about Michael's family? Does he have brothers and sisters?"

"No," Claire said. "But he has a mother. I'd like it if you asked her. Michael doesn't talk about her much, but I'm sure she's up to the trip."

"Is she ill?" Ellen asked.

"I don't think so, but . . . you know . . ." Claire broke off.

Ellen was puzzled by Claire's attitude, but decided not to pursue the subject. The date for the reception was set for the Saturday after next and Ellen ordered invitations.

Michael was pleased when Claire told him that his mother was invited and called her immediately. Claire got on the phone too, and Mrs. Shea said she would be "overjoyed to meet Claire and stay for a visit. But no moah than a week."

After they'd finished talking, Claire said, "Your mother sounds like a very sweet person. She's quite southern, isn't she?"

"She is. I'm sure you'll like her."

Michael's mother arrived by train the following Friday afternoon. Michael managed to get away from the hospital early enough to meet her. He told Claire not to bother going with him—the train would probably be late.

Claire grew a little edgy waiting for them. She'd rearranged the bedroom Mrs. Shea would use, trying to make it more convenient for an older person. She'd selected the dinner menu with care too. Nothing too highly seasoned, nothing salty.

She heard a car stop and hurried to the front door. Michael and his mother were coming up the steps. Could that be his mother? She looked so young! Brown hair, untinged by gray, curled around the edges of a perky mink hat. Claire was aware of shapely legs and tiny, thin-heeled pumps. The woman looked adorable, and Claire hated her on sight.

Mrs. Shea ignored Claire's outstretched hand and stood on tiptoe to kiss her. "So you're Michael Junior's wife! I've been dying to meet you."

Claire stepped back. "Mrs. Shea! It's lovely to meet you."

"Call me Marvel." She saw Claire's look of surprise. "My daddy named me that. He took one look at me when I was born and said, 'We'll call her Marvel 'cause that's just what she is.'"

Claire didn't understand every word. Could anyone be named "Mahvul"? Maybe she'd said Mabel. Until she was sure, Claire decided to call her "You."

Marvel gazed at the spacious entrance hall, clasping her delicate hands as though in prayer. "How beautiful this is. All my life, I've dreamed of Michael Junior living in a house like this."

Claire glanced at Michael. His face was ashen.

"Won't you come with me?" Claire said. "I'll show you to your room. And when you're ready, you can see the rest of the house."

Poor Michael! Claire understood him much better now. She could even overlook certain traits of his that bothered her. To be brought up by a barricuda in butterfly's wings!

Claire smiled in sympathy and excused herself. Let Michael take over!

Claire, Michael, and Marvel arrived a few minutes early for the party at Ellen and David's. Within the hour, the other invited guests arrived. Claire looked particularly well, Ellen thought, in a lovely soft blue wool, something from her new couturier wardrobe. Michael had insisted on it. Claire thought it was a little matronly, too much like the things she'd been wearing for years.

Sandy and Bob came to the party, bringing Jimmy and Tom with them. Jimmy was home from Yale for semester break. Nancy and Chris came, and a number of staff people from Memorial Hospital. Dan brought a date, Susan Burke. But for the most part, the guests were long-time friends of Claire's.

Marvel Shea had a wonderful time. She was outgoing and interested in everyone she met. The young people danced and Marvel danced too, never lacking for a partner. "I love to fox-trot," she told Jimmy McGuire.

Claire watched Michael dancing. He's so lithe, so graceful. She could never dance that well, even when she was young. The thought startled her. She mustn't think this way. Michael was dancing with the girl who came with Jimmy. What was her name? Oh, yes, Jennifer something-or-other. They danced without touching. Jennifer was wearing a silver lamé sheath that seemed to flow around her as she moved. Michael was watching her, looking into her eyes, smiling. What was he thinking? Claire looked away for a moment. Someone might notice her staring and think she was jealous of Michael. When she looked again, they were gone. Had they gone outside? Claire thought she'd go out too. Fresh air would be nice. She'd go out and have a cigarette.

Claire went into the library. There was no one there. She opened the door and stepped out onto the side porch. No one here either. She lit her cigarette and leaned against a pillar. Then she noticed a figure in the porch swing. "Who is it? I can't see a thing, it's so dark."

"It's Tom Hughes, Mrs. Cassen. I mean . . ."

"I know, Tom. It's all right. But what are you doing out here? Why aren't you inside dancing?"

"I can't do that stuff," Tom said.

Claire laughed. "Neither can I and I'm too old to learn." Tom didn't say anything so she tried again. "How's school?"

"It's okay. Mrs. Shea, do you mind if I ask you something?"

"Not at all," Claire said.

"Did you ever know my mother?"

"Lisa? Of course." *That wretched girl*, Claire thought. *I hope he doesn't ask me anything about her.* She wondered what good things she could say about an amoral little creep.

"I saw her today."

"You did!"

"Yeah. And you know what? She didn't even recognize me."

Claire couldn't think of a tactful or comforting observation to make. "Tom, it's cold out here. Let's go inside and get something to eat."

"Okay. I saw some chocolate cake in the kitchen." Tom got up and started for the door, and Claire followed him.

They walked in silence through the empty library and down the hall into the kitchen. Michael appeared to be startled, and Jennifer's face was flushed when Claire and Tom came into the room.

"Claire!" Michael said. "Where have you been?"

"Out," Claire answered. "Tom and I are looking for cake." She barged into a cabinet in her hurry to get away. She should have worn her glasses! What was he doing in the kitchen with that girl? Couldn't she let him out of her sight for even one minute! Scared and furious, Claire returned to the living room. Good! There was Ellen with a group of friends. She'd join them.

Claire got through the rest of the evening somehow. Michael was by her side most of the time, touching her hand, putting his arm around her shoulders, and in general behaving like an ardent bridegroom.

Claire, Michael, and Marvel were the last guests to leave the party. As they rode home, Marvel went on and on about the wonderful time she'd had, the charm of their friends, the graciousness of their hosts.

Claire would have believed her if she hadn't seen the expression in Marvel's eyes, watchful and hard and cold. But Claire was too tired for a continuing encounter with her mother-in-law. Excusing herself, she went to her room. Because of his uncertain hours at the hospital, Michael had moved into a room down the hall.

Claire slept fitfully. Once she was awakened by the sound of voices raised in anger. Listening intently, she thought she heard Marvel say, "And now you're going to mess this up too." Michael answered, but his voice was too low for Claire to hear and she slept again.

When Claire woke up, Michael had already left for the hospital. She had breakfast alone with Marvel. As usual, Marvel was looking fresh and beautiful. She talked a blue streak. "I'm just as sorry as I can be, but I have to go home. My next-door neighbor and my dearest friend—she's the same person of course—called me this morning and said I just must get back there for the church bazaar. I'm the chairman, you know, and so many things have come up that need my attention."

Claire tried to stem Marvel's flow of conversation

but finally gave up. She assured Marvel that she'd take her to the train. Two hours later, the mission accomplished and Marvel enroute back to where she'd come from, Claire went home and back to bed.

Later that day, Michael called to say that he wouldn't be home for dinner. They talked a little about his mother, how sorry they were that she had to leave, and Michael hung up.

Well here I am with nothing to do again, Claire thought. *Just like the old days.* On the other hand, she might be frightening him away. Perhaps he was hurt, thinking that she'd suspected him of something. So what if he'd kissed that Jennifer in the kitchen. Her eyes had been wide open when she'd married a much younger man. They had something going between them that was a lot more important then sex. And maybe Michael was upset because she hadn't done anything about establishing a personal income for him, as she'd promised. She'd get on that right away. Claire went to the phone and dialed Chris Hughes' office.

Michael had a rough day, most of it in surgery. He hated it. On days like this he wondered why in hell he'd become a doctor. He knew why—his darling little mother. Well, thank God she'd left. Such a strain being around her! Claire had handled her, though! She'd been as nice as pie, just like Mama. It was early yet and it'd be a long evening at home. Michael thought he'd drop by the club for one drink and see who was around.

He drove up to the entrance and got out of his Porsche, handing the keys to the attendant. On his way into the bar, he paused by the mirror, smoothing his hair close to his head. Good thing he didn't look as frazzled as he felt. He walked into the Oak Room and sat on a bar stool.

"Hi, Hank! Jack Daniels and no rocks." He was aware of someone beside him.

"Hi, do you come here often?"

Michael turned to see a girl with a gamin face, crowned by elaborately combed titian hair. She took his breath away. He could feel his mouth twisting into a foolish grin.

"Cat got your tongue?" the girl asked.

"Have we met?" Michael countered.

"Not yet, but we're about to. I'm Lisa Miller. That was my first name and I've just gone back to it. I've had a lot of other names in between." She picked the olive out of her glass and popped it in her mouth. "Aren't the olives wonderful after they've soaked in gin and that other stuff?"

"Does your mother know you're drinking martinis?"

Lisa gave him a blank look.

"And does she know you're wearing her clothes?"

Lisa looked down at her severely cut black satin, and on down to her black nylons and black satin pumps. Then she grinned. "You should see what Mother wears. Hey! You never did tell me your name."

"I'm Michael Shea."

"Aha!" Lisa said. "You're the bridegroom. I've heard a lot about you."

"And I've heard a lot about you. You used to be married to Bob Hughes."

"That's right! I did. But he was two husbands ago. I have a brand-new divorce. Want to see my decree?"

"Later! You're about dry there. Would you like another?"

Lisa nodded her head and sat back on her stool, studying Michael. "You're even more handsome than they say."

"They're too kind. How long do you plan to be in Oakdale?"

Lisa shrugged. "I just signed a lease for a house." She gave him a solemn look. "I'm your new neighbor."

"You are?"

"I'm moving into the Farleys' gatehouse."

"Well that's great." Michael's voice sounded hollow, even to himself. This lady could be trouble. "You'll be near your ex-husband's house. Bob Hughes is on the next block."

Lisa's face brightened. "I know that. Do you think I can borrow a cup of sugar?" She slipped forward, bracing herself with her elbow.

"Maybe you should have a cup of coffee instead of a martini."

"You've been married too long!" Lisa rapped the bar with her fist. "You sound just like Claire."

"Then you're acquainted with my wife."

Lisa sat up straight, wrinkling her nose. "Sure!"

Michael laughed. "You sound just like her. Maybe you'd like me to take you home?"

Lisa tossed her head. "Maybe I would! After one more drink to ease a mother's aching heart."

Michael was laughing again. "Whose mother's aching heart?"

Lisa put down her glass and stared into it. "My son's mother's aching heart."

Michael began to fidget. Female drunks got on his nerves. And this one was going to start crying or worse. He wanted to get out of her way before she did either. "If you're sure I can't do anything for you?" He hoped she'd forgotten that he was there and he could get away.

Lisa adjusted the black satin pillbox on her head

and beamed. "You may drive me home! For the time being, I'm house-sitting for friends who're out of town. And I'm lonely."

Michael was confused. All at once the woman was entirely sober. He'd been had. But the evening ahead seemed promising. He took her arm. "Shall we?"

Lisa looked into his eyes and walked with him to his car.

Chapter Twelve
. . . And An End

Michael drove leisurely in the direction of the address Lisa had given him. Even though he was eager to be in bed with her, he wanted to anticipate his pleasure.

Lisa leaned back against the seat, looking out at Oakdale. Occasionally she smiled. Once she waved at someone in a passing car. "I love being back here," she murmured. "How do you like being married to an older woman?"

"There are certain advantages." And as an afterthought, he added, "And drawbacks." Michael glanced at Lisa. "How did you like bedtime with your old husband?"

Ignoring his question, Lisa leaned forward and turned on the radio. She turned the dial until she found a station with rock music. Then she turned up the volume. "I saw my son today." She tapped her foot in time to the rhythm. "He was such a beautiful baby. But now what an ugly boy!" She closed her eyes.

Women, Michael thought. He wished he could live without them! And mothers were the worst kinds of women. Look at this one. She was desirable, not beautiful exactly, but he wanted her. And she was trouble! What if someone should see them? Claire would kick him out for sure. He'd damn near blown it last night when he kissed that dull little girl. Michael wondered how his mother had found out. She sure raised hell with him about it. He grinned at the memory.

"Why are you laughing?" Lisa asked.

"How much farther?" Michael asked. He had nothing to tell Lisa. Furthermore, he didn't intend to see her again after tonight.

"Turn here and park in the garage. The door's open," Lisa said.

He kissed her when they were in the garage. Her throat was firm, and she smelled faintly of musk.

Lisa was beginning to writhe. "Come on," she said, "let's go into the bedroom." She opened the car door and eased herself out.

As she was unlocking the door leading into the house from the garage, Michael glanced around. One of these new split levels proliferating the landscape. So new and so modest, he thought. Compared to this, his and Claire's house was a jewel. Lisa had opened the door. Yelling, she ran through the house, taking her clothes off as she went. For a second, Michael was surprised. Then he was running down the hall after her.

Being with Lisa made him realize how hungry he'd been for a young, lusty woman. At first he was too eager and Lisa complained. "Well, really!"

"Don't pout," Michael said. "I can do better." He did.

Afterward Lisa fell into a deep sleep. He watched her for a while. She was so beautiful, he thought. Lisa was a woman of no pretenses and no reserve. They were a great pair. When he kissed her goodbye, she hardly stirred. He left, locking the door behind him, and raced the car all the way home.

Claire heard him drive into the garage and decided to say nothing. She'd wait and see. Next morning they chatted all through breakfast and made plans for the evening. Claire decided that she was a worrywart. She should relax and enjoy life.

Michael began his day with high resolves to avoid Lisa in the future. He'd be good to Claire, make love to her at suitable intervals, and attend to business.

Then Lisa called him early that afternoon. "Would you be coming by tonight?" she asked.

Michael's manner was businesslike. "Can't talk now," he said. "There's someone here." He was alone in his office, but it would have been a mistake to carry on a conversation.

That night Claire and Michael went to dinner in a new French restaurant. After the waiter had taken their order, Claire said, "We have a new neighbor."

"Oh?" Michael said cautiously, "Which house?"

"A woman who lived in Oakdale a few years ago has leased the Farleys' gatehouse."

"Do you know her?"

"Yes." Claire almost growled. "She's calling herself Miller now. It's her maiden name, I think. She's Tom Hughes' mother, heaven help him!"

"I guess she was before my time," Michael said. "How's your sole?"

"Lovely," Claire said. "I can't imagine why the creature wants to come back to Oakdale. She's totally unethical. In fact, she's a terrible woman. I talked to Nancy today, and she's fit to be tied."

"That's too bad," Michael mumbled. He wished

Claire would talk about something else. "We don't need to have anything to do with her, do we?"

"I certainly don't intend to. It's time we entertained. Is Saturday night good for you?"

"Great!" Thank God! She was off the subject of Lisa.

As the weeks passed, Michael found himself thinking of Lisa more and more. He knew when she moved into the gatehouse. The lights were always on, no matter how late he drove by. He knew she slept late in the morning because there was never a sign of life when he passed on the way to the hospital. He wondered if she were seeing anyone. She must be! Thinking of her in bed with someone else irritated him. He'd better get hold of himself.

One morning as he passed the house, he noticed that her car wasn't there. Where would a late-riser like Lisa go at eight o'clock?

He was a little late in getting to the hospital. As he hurried into his office, his secretary looked up. "Your patient is waiting, doctor."

"Sorry," Michael said. "I didn't realize I had an early appointment."

"You didn't. But the patient called after you'd left the hospital yesterday afternoon. She sounded so desperate that I . . ."

"That's quite all right, Edna. What's her name?"

Edna glanced at the appointment book. "She's a Miss Miller, she says. But she looks familiar. I think she used to be Mrs. Hughes."

"Thank you, Edna." Michael walked into his office and carefully closed the door. Damn her. What in hell did she want? He looked at Lisa, fighting to keep from taking her in his arms. "Miss Miller?"

"You got it, Doc."

"And how are you feeling today?" He'd better sound professional, he thought. Nosy Edna might have her ear to the door.

"I'm feeling fine, doctor."

Lisa was simpering, and he wanted to wring her neck. "Why did you wish to see me?"

"I think you know the answer to that, doctor. I wish to hop into bed with you."

Michael cleared his throat. "Lisa, please! Someone may hear you. Now be serious, what are you here to see me about?"

Lisa's eyes glinted with anger. "I'm pregnant, you idiot!"

Michael gasped. "Then see an OB! I'm a plastic surgeon."

Lisa was laughing now. "I've seen an obstetrician and I'm three months pregnant. Don't you remember? And what are you going to do about it?"

Michael could feel the blood draining from his body. This was the end of everything for him. "No! I don't remember! What are you going to do about this? Naturally, I know someone who can terminate the pregnancy."

"Of course you do," she said bitterly. "But I want this baby and you're going to divorce Claire and marry me!"

"The hell I will!" Michael knew he was shouting. Better get a hold on himself. "How do I know this is my baby?"

"I know!" Lisa said. "And you'll find out when I take you to court."

"You can forget the whole thing, Lisa. I won't divorce Claire and I don't want to be a father. Now get out of here. I don't want you to call me ever." He walked out the office. He saw Edna's expression. She'd heard everything! Now everybody in the hospital would know. Was that bitch Lisa actually pregnant? A woman of her age and with her sexual history. Well, it was a setup!

Claire noticed his uneasiness. "What's wrong with you, Michael?" she asked. "You look terrible. Are you sick?"

"No, no, dear. I'm fine. Don't worry about me."

"But I do worry," Claire said. "I think you're working too hard."

That night when she was in bed, Michael came into her room to make love to her. It was like the first time. Life was rich and full again.

At breakfast the next morning, Claire said, "Did I tell you? I'm playing in the golf tournament at the club."

"No, you didn't tell me," Michael said. "Enjoy yourself and bring home the bacon." He kissed her and went into his room to dress.

Claire called after him. "I may be late getting home this afternoon. You know how these things can go."

"I know," Michael said. "Have a good game." He blew her a kiss and left by the side door.

What a beautiful day, Claire thought. And perfect for golf. The sun was shining, there was a nip in the air, and not a trace of a breeze to send a ball off course. All at once Claire wanted to see Ellen and talk to her. *I'm being silly*, she thought, but she called her anyway.

The beauty of the day didn't cheer Michael. He felt tense and cross. For no reason at all, he bawled out Edna. He was sorry afterward and tried to apologize. It wasn't smart to make an enemy of Edna, the woman who knew too much. He went downstairs to the coffee shop and sat at a table with David and Bob.

David said, "You're looking a little seedy, Michael. Why don't you knock off early and go home? You look like you need sleep."

"I think I will, doctor."

Michael left the hospital about four. He turned his head as he drove past the gatehouse. Lisa was the last person he wanted to see today. He'd never killed anybody, but Lisa tempted him. If he thought he could get away with it, he might try. He yawned. David was right. He needed sleep. Michael drove into the garage and closed the door. As he was walking into the house, he saw Lisa coming through the little grove of trees that separated their property from the Farleys'. Christ! She was heading this way. He went into the house too late. She'd seen him.

"Michael!"

Thank God! Claire wasn't home. He'd get Lisa out of the house before Claire got back. "What do you want?"

"I want to talk to you," Lisa yelled back. She came into the house and he slammed the door behind her. "My! My!" she said. "I had no idea you were so grand. Squire Shea, the Lord of the Manor."

"What do you want, Lisa?" He looked at his watch. "I'll give you two minutes. Then you'll have to go!"

Lisa batted her eyelashes. "Gracious! Aren't you going to ask me to sit?"

"No! What do you want, Lisa?"

"I want a father for my unborn child! That's what I want."

I must keep calm, he thought. "Lisa, why do you want to have this child? You're a rotten mother. Women like you have no right to have children."

Lisa slumped against the wall. "I know that," she moaned. "Tom hates me. I want a baby who'll love me." She covered her face with her hands, trying to stifle her sobs.

The sight of her disgusted Michael. How could he ever have wanted her, made love to her? She was disgusting with her bloated red face and her nagging manner. "Lisa, just get out of here. I don't want this kid and I don't want you! I'll never give this up." He lifted Lisa to her feet and pushed her toward the door and pulled it open.

Lisa was yelling, "Let go of me!" He did, abruptly.

With a jolt, he had realized the front door was open; he pushed in front of Lisa. Claire's glasses were on the steps. But where was Claire? When did she get home? "Claire!" he yelled. "Where are you, Claire?" He waited for an answer and then he began to run. He ran across the yard and down the driveway to the road, calling her name over and over. Then he saw her far ahead, and almost to the highway. He called again. "Claire! Wait for me, Claire."

She must have heard him. She looked back once, then hurried on.

Michael yelled, "Claire, come back. You left your glasses on the steps. You can't see where you're going."

If she heard him, she was ignoring him, because she kept running. Then she was crossing the highway, looking neither right nor left. Michael was closer to her now, near enough to hear the roar of traffic. But Claire wouldn't stop. "Claire!" His voice was hoarse. Of course she couldn't hear him now and she was in the third lane.

Michael saw the big truck bearing down on her. Claire couldn't get out of the way, even if she knew it was there. He heard grinding gears and saw the truck sway, and Claire vanished.

The Highway Patrol reached Claire before Michael.

She was pinned under the wheels, but she was still breathing.

Michael rode to the hospital in a patrol car. There was no need for him to call Ellen. David already had. He didn't want to see Ellen anyway. She'd know everything was his fault. What could he say that would explain why a woman with everything to live for would throw herself under a truck?

Marvel Shea arrived in Oakdale that night. "I came to be with my boy in his time of need," she told everyone within earshot. He dreaded the hour when she'd turn on him, saying, "You really messed up, didn't you, Michael Junior? I knew you would! Remember, I told you you would."

Claire's neck had been broken in the accident. But she continued to live without gaining consciousness. Scans showed some activity in the brain. Despite everything that David said, Ellen went on hoping that her mother would recover.

As the weeks passed into months, Michael wanted Claire to die. The sight of her body, gouged with needles and tubes, was horrifying. And as long as she was alive, people kept asking, "Why did she do it?" Maybe if she died, people would forget to ask.

Lisa was having problems of her own. As her pregnancy grew more obvious, the gossip increased.

One day Tom drove to Lisa's house and knocked on the door. Lisa invited him in and offered him a cola.

"Thanks, lady," Tom said. "But I'd like something stronger."

"But, Tom, you're not even eighteen. Surely you don't drink."

"Are you kidding, lady?" Tom threw himself on the sofa and stared at her. Finally he said, "Some mother!" and got up to go.

"Wait, Tom! Where are you going?"

"Out of here. I've seen enough. And I'm really sorry for your next kid." He ran out of the house and jumped into his car. He didn't want her to see him crying.

Lisa put her head back and stared at the ceiling. Michael and now Tom! Both of them said she had no right to have this baby. But she'd have him and he'd be all hers. This time she'd do it right. This baby was going to love her! He'd never look at her the way Tom did just now. And he wouldn't have a father. But that didn't matter.

Lisa thought of Claire. She guessed maybe Claire was partly her fault. A lot her fault. And she'd probably pay for it. But it didn't matter, just as long as the baby was all right!

Chapter Thirteen
New Life

Ellen went to the hospital to be with her mother twice a day, sometimes more. David tried to talk her out of going so often, but she wouldn't listen. By now Claire was almost unrecognizable, a frightful skeleton of the vibrant woman she had been. Ellen would sit beside her bed in intensive care for as long as she was allowed, holding Claire's hand, searching her face for a sign of recognition.

Late one afternoon, six months from the day of the accident, as Ellen sat beside Claire's bed, she felt a slight pressure on her hand and saw Claire's eyelids flutter. That was all.

David, who had been watching the monitor over Claire's bed, put his arms around Ellen and lifted her to her feet. "It's over. Time to leave now, dear."

Ellen sagged against him, allowing herself to be led from the room. She was relieved that everything was over. Someday she'd forget this poor shadow of her mother. The nightmare would fade and be replaced by loving memory. But not yet. And here was Michael, racing toward them down the corridor. She turned her head—she couldn't look at him when she still hated him so much.

Michael made all the arrangements for Claire's funeral. Ellen told herself she didn't care. He was Claire's husband! Let him take care of everything. He had Claire's money now. Let him earn his keep.

The funeral was at the graveside and brief. Besides Ellen and her family, only Claire's closest and dearest friends were there—Nancy, Chris, Bob and Sandy, and Tom, some cousins of Claire's. That was about it.

For Michael the service was incredibly long and totally unbearable. He had to get back to the hospital. Lisa had checked in around eight that morning. She must be in deep labor by now, or maybe the baby had been born! He should be at the hospital, checking on Lisa, finding out what she was saying. But he couldn't get away. He had to stand shivering in the cold, wet wind on a treeless hill. Marvel was at his side, demure and beautiful in billowing black chiffon.

When the service was over, the mourners left in small groups, walking slowly to their cars. No one spoke.

Marvel clutched Michael's arm to keep from falling. She found it hard to walk on soggy ground in high heels. "Don't walk so fast, honey." Her voice carried all the way down the hill to where the cars were parked. "I can't get this out of my mind. There's poor Claire, less than a year older than me, lying dead in her grave. It just makes you wonder."

Michael didn't answer. He had to get her back to his house on Country Club Lane and hurry to the hospital. He hoped his mother would leave town soon.

On his return to the hospital, Michael made a few discreet inquiries and learned that Lisa had delivered an eight-pound boy by Cesarian section. He was not elated. The baby was her problem. It was a boy—he found he was curious as to what it looked like.

Everyone, or almost everyone, was polite and kind to Michael that day. After all, he was a bereaved husband, going on with his life in a subdued, gallant way. At least that was the image he tried to project. He could ease up a bit in a few weeks and openly start going out with women, no more sneaking around.

He'd seen quite a bit of Lorraine in recent months. Lorraine had forgiven him for getting married. She even felt a little sorry for him. "To think the society dame he'd married was nuts." That was Lorraine's version, and Michael fed her bits of information to bolster her beliefs.

As the day wore on, Michael occasionally thought of that new baby in the nursery. He guessed there was no harm in looking at the kid. Lisa would be leaving the hospital in a few days, and he'd never see the little guy again.

The next morning Michael happened to be on the fifth floor maternity ward. On impulse he stopped at the nursery and glanced through the big glass window. There was his kid, yelling his head off. God! What a husky boy. Look at those shoulders! He was something.

"Isn't he darling?"

Michael started. Edna was at his side, giving him a knowing look. "Which one? They all look like babies to me." Michael tried to sound casual.

"I was talking about the redheaded one, the Miller baby. He has hair the color of yours. Isn't that odd!"

"I don't know. His mother has red hair, doesn't she?" Michael walked away. Let her think what she wanted, but she'd better keep her mouth shut. Lately he'd been keeping a file on Edna. He'd collected a few tidbits she wouldn't like to have broadcast.

Lisa didn't see her baby until the day after he was born. But he was worth waiting for. Lisa was sure he was the most remarkable baby ever born.

After the nurse had placed the baby in Lisa's arms, she asked, "What will you name him?"

Lisa could hardly see his face, her eyes were so misty. "Charles, I think. After my father." Lisa giggled. "Look at that big nose!"

"He'll grow into that," the nurse said.

Lisa bent to kiss his forehead. "Charles doesn't really suit him, though, do you think? I'll call him Chuck!"

"He looks like a Chuck," the nurse said. "Now I'll leave you two to get better-acquainted." She knew that Lisa hadn't heard a word she'd said. That was one of the reasons she loved working in maternity. The mothers were almost as wonderful as the babies.

Chuck nursed for a little and went to sleep. Lisa, feeling secure and contented, closed her eyes. Then she felt a hand clamping her shoulder.

"You! You're asleep. What kind of mother are you, sleeping while holding your infant!" a voice said coolly.

"Wait just a minute!" Lisa sat up straighter and stared at the rather plain-looking young woman in a white coat. "Who are you and how dare you talk to me this way!"

"I'm Dr. Burke, the resident on duty." She reached for Chuck, but Lisa held on. "Give him to me, Miss Miller. It's time for the babies to be back in the nursery."

With misgivings, Lisa let the doctor have the baby. "I thought that nice nurse would be coming back for him."

"Nelson! I expect she's gone off duty." Dr. Burke's thin lips stretched into a faint smile. "Now don't go back to sleep, Miss Miller. I'll be back to talk to you."

Burke, Smurke, whatever her name is, I don't like her, Lisa decided. And here she was back again. "That didn't take long, doctor. How do you get around so fast? Do you use roller skates?" Lisa glanced down at the sensible white flats attached to the doctor's thick ankles. "I guess you're built for it."

Dr. Burke bit her lower lip. "Do you plan on giving your baby up for adoption, *Miss Miller?*"

"No, I'm not giving my baby up for adoption," Lisa said, imitating the other woman's voice.

"I believe you misunderstand me," Dr. Burke said. "We're only trying to help you. As an unmarried woman, you might find caring for a baby difficult."

Lisa fluffed the pale blue ostrich feathers that bordered her bed jacket. "I know who you are, doctor. You're Susan Burke and you're after Dan Stewart. But I don't think you know who I am. And when you do find out, you're going to be damn sorry you ever spoke to me. Now will you get the hell out of here!"

After Susan left her room, Lisa began to make hurried preparations to leave the hospital. Through an agency, she was able to hire a nurse to care for the baby. She could manage everything else on her own. Two days later, Lisa was back at the gatehouse and happy to be there.

During the first week at home, no one came to call. But Lisa didn't mind. She loved being alone with the baby. Nurse Simpson was a comforting presence, and she didn't intrude.

When Chuck was eight days old, Tom came to see him. Lisa was pleased. "Why, Tom! I'm so glad you're here."

"Yeah? I, uh, I was down the road and kind of wanted to see my half-brother."

"I'm glad." Lisa kissed him lightly on the cheek. "He makes me think of you. In here!" She grabbed his hand and pulled him into the bedroom.

Tom looked at the baby for a long minute. "Thanks," he said and walked toward the front door.

"But, Tom! Can't you stay for a while? I want to talk to you."

"No. Gotta go!"

Lisa watched Tom cut across the postage-stamp-sized front yard and vault over the car door into the driver's seat. She heard the motor start and saw the car shoot away out of sight. *Now why wouldn't he stay and talk to me?* she asked herself. *Why is he like this?* She went back into the house, thinking Bob hadn't done a very good job bringing up their son.

To Michael's great relief, his mother stayed for less than a week after Claire's funeral. A cleaning woman came three times a week, but he rarely saw her. In fact, he found living alone a bit lonely.

Lisa, in the gatehouse, was out of sight of his house, but rarely out of his mind. There she was living alone and with his baby, less than a quarter of a mile away. Maybe he was a fool, but he would like to see that kid again. Now that Claire was gone, why not? Maybe if Lisa was still determined to marry him, he might think about it. After a decent interval of course. It wouldn't look good for him to remarry too soon.

Each time he passed the gatehouse, Michael took a quick look to see if Lisa had company. He rarely saw a car other than Lisa's parked near the house.

One Sunday morning he dressed with particular care and strolled down to Lisa's place. The house was small, but charming, he thought. It matched the huge English manorhouse the Farley family had built in the early twenties.

Lisa was answering the doorbell, he could hear her heels clicking on the parquet floor. The door swung open and Lisa was glaring at him. "What do you want, Michael?"

He'd planned to say something flippant about being neighbors, but the haunted expression in her eyes stopped him cold. "I . . . how are you?"

"I'm fine," she snapped. "Anything else?"

Michael walked past her into the living room. "Where is he? I want to see him."

Lisa stepped in front of him, as though trying to block his way. "He's asleep."

"Well, could I just look at him? I won't wake him up."

Michael didn't know why, but Lisa gave in. "Okay," she said. "But be very quiet. I don't want him to wake up too soon from his nap." On tiptoe, she led Michael into the bedroom.

Michael bent over to see his son more clearly. The copper-colored hair was considerably longer than it was at his birth. Now it waved softly like a cap on his well-shaped head. "He's beautiful." Michael's voice was husky.

"He's healthy. That's the most important thing," Lisa said briskly.

"Aren't you afraid of waking him?" Michael asked in a whisper.

Lisa flushed. "He's a good sleeper. But we'd better leave him now."

Damn her, Michael thought. He detested this woman. Why wouldn't she get out of the way and leave him alone with his son? Lisa was standing outside the door, waiting for him to leave the room.

After one last look, he followed her out.

When Lisa didn't ask him to sit down, he said, "How about a cup of coffee?"

Lisa frowned in annoyance. "There may be a little left in the pot. But it'll be cold."

"That's all right. Pour it over ice and I'll have iced coffee." He sat down to wait.

Lisa gritted her teeth, then flounced out of the room.

Michael could hear her muttering in the little kitchen. Evidently she was having trouble getting ice cubes out of the tray. He sat back, smiling in satisfaction. If he were to have his son, he'd have to take the mother too. He crossed his legs and studied his Italian loafers. Perhaps he should scuff them a bit—Claire had taught him to avoid the nouveau look.

Ah, Lisa was back with his coffee. He reached for the glass, but she bypassed him and slammed it on the table beside him, spilling the liquid.

Lisa went to stand in front of the bedroom door. "Let's get to the point, Michael. What do you want?"

"I want you, Lisa." He stood up and started toward her, planning to take her in his arms.

"Get out! And don't you ever come here again!" Her voice was shaking with anger.

"You can't stop me, Lisa! I have a right to see my son."

Lisa took a step toward him. "He's not your son! Now get out of here."

Lisa was still coming toward him, holding her right hand behind her. Did she have a knife? Michael backed away from her and toward the door. "All right, Lisa. I'll leave now, but I'm coming back. With a court order, if necessary."

After that he tried a new tactic, sending gifts to

Chuck. He selected beautiful, handmade gowns and rompers, an antique walnut cradle, imported toys, everything he could think of, and had them all delivered to Lisa's house. The next time he dropped by for a visit, she wouldn't let him in.

Although his courtship of Lisa was floundering, his relationship with Lorraine was thriving. Many nights he didn't go home. Instead he stayed with Lorraine in the large roomy apartment he had leased for her. And it was convenient to the hospital.

One night Michael was sitting at his special table at Lorraine's club, waiting for her to go on, when Lisa came in with an escort. The sight of her made him furious. Who was staying with the baby? He was about to go to her table and ask when the lights dimmed and the spotlight hit Lorraine. He'd wait until Lorraine's number was over.

He didn't make his move quickly enough because Lorraine appeared before her theme music had faded and made a big show of kissing him. As soon as she got out of his way, he looked for Lisa. She'd seen the whole thing—he could tell by the smug expression on her face.

The next day as he was preparing to stop at Lisa's house, he noticed a car parked by her door. It was probably the oaf he'd seen her with last night, he decided, and drove on.

Michael saw the car often after that, and he was worried. What if Lisa got married? Being Chuck's biological father wasn't good enough. He had to establish the relationship legally.

He called Lisa from his office. "Lisa," he said when he heard her voice, "I'd like to stop by for a few minutes this evening."

"I won't be at home."

"Then perhaps I can see Chuck. Please instruct the sitter." That gambit would get her, Michael reasoned.

"Well"— Lisa sounded hesitant—"all right if you won't stay long. I'll be home early in the evening, but then I'm taking Chuckie out of town for the weekend."

"Thank you. That will be fine." Michael put down the phone.

He rang Lisa's doorbell promptly at seven. When she let him into the house, she seemed a little too assured. Michael wondered if someone were in the house with her to offer the protection she might imagine she needed.

Michael came straight to the point. "Lisa, I want to marry you. We're Chuck's parents and we should be married."

Lisa crossed her long legs, smoothing her skirt. "That could be," she purred. "But not necessarily to one another."

He wanted to strangle her. "Lisa, I love you. And I love Chuck. He's my son."

"How strange to hear you talk this way, Michael. I remember a very different attitude expressed by you. And rudely."

"Things were very different then, as you damn well know. I had a wife and responsibilities toward her."

"Funny, I never noticed."

Michael gave up and went home. The next morning as he passed the gatehouse on his way to the hospital, he saw a moving van backed up to the front door. He wondered where she was going. Was she leaving town? He had ways of finding out.

Chapter Fourteen
Off Again, On Again

Dan Stewart sat at his accustomed table in Memorial Hospital's coffee shop, stirring his tea. "Susan, you really surprised me when you accepted the appointment."

"Why were you surprised? I like Oakdale and I like Memorial." Susan shrugged her square shoulders. "Maybe I really like you."

They talked for a while and then they drove to his parents' house so he could pick up a suit he needed. On the way, Susan asked him to marry her. He was shocked. He knew she cared about him more than he cared about her, though Susan had never seemed capable of much emotion except sexual. But marriage—he wasn't ready for that, and not with Susan.

"I don't know, Susan," he said. "I don't know . . ."

He turned into his parents' driveway, glad for the chance to put off talking about marriage. It was a welcome relief.

Ellen met them in the hall. "Dan," she said, kissing his cheek. "And Susan! It's nice to see you."

Susan threw her arms around Ellen's neck. "Oh, Mrs. Stewart, we have exciting news!" she cried, ignoring Dan's restraining hand on her shoulder.

"What is your news?" Ellen asked.

"It's too soon . . ."

Susan's voice drowned out Dan's. "Dan and I are getting married!"

Ellen's smile seemed strained, Dan thought. "This is a surprise. I think I'll sit down." Ellen sank into a chair. "Does your father know about this?"

"Not yet," Dan said.

"We just found out ourselves. I'm so happy. Do you mind if I call Mom and Dad?"

Before Ellen could answer, Susan was dialing the hall phone. Ellen looked at Dan and saw the stunned expression in his eyes. "When's the wedding?" she asked.

Dan shrugged and shook his head.

An hour after Dan and Susan had left, David came home. He put his coat in the closet and went into the living room to lie on the sofa. When Ellen came in, he said, "I hope we don't have anything planned for tonight. I'm bushed."

Ellen sat across from David. She hated to bother him. Maybe he should take a nap before dinner. Still she felt she had to say something. "David, did you talk to Dan today?"

"I saw him late this morning. Why?" David closed his eyes.

"Well, he and Susan stopped by here this afternoon. And Susan said they were engaged."

David sat up slowly and looked at Ellen. "Susan said? Well what did Dan say?"

"He didn't deny it. David, what do you think of Susan?"

David thought for a second. "She's intelligent," he

said slowly. "I think she'll make a fine internist, if she can develop a better manner around patients. I guess you heard about the run-in she had . . ." He remembered in time not to mention Lisa's name.

"With whom?" Ellen asked.

"Oh, it was just some patient at the hospital. The woman was furious. It's a wonder she didn't sue. Actually Susan would do very well in research, or some other area where a bedside manner isn't required."

"But do you like Susan?" Ellen persisted.

"Like her? Sure. She's all right."

"I'm sure she is. But I'm not sure she's right for Dan."

"Maybe she isn't," David said. "But I'm damned if I know how to stop it."

"I don't think we're very good at stopping unsuitable marriages," Ellen mused, remembering their efforts to keep Claire from marrying Michael. "I'll see about dinner," she said and went to the kitchen.

Susan and Dan were married in an exclusive country club on Chicago's North Shore. A lavish reception followed. Ellen, David, and Paul were guests, as were a few friends of the bridal couple from Memorial Hospital.

After a brief honeymoon in the south of France, the bride and groom returned to Oakdale to the pleasant apartment Susan had found for them before the wedding.

Dan couldn't see any change in his life style. He and Susan had been living together before they got married, and they continued to work together, just as they had for several years. He wasn't bored exactly, but sometimes he wished that something interesting would happen.

Then Dan met Liz Talbot.

Dan was working in Emergency when Liz was

brought in on a stretcher. She had been riding in a car that was struck from the rear, and was suffering from whiplash and a possible concussion. Dan treated her and made the arrangements to admit her to the hospital.

The next morning, he went to see her. From her chart he learned that she had been born in Surrey and had lived in London for the past five years. She was twenty-two and at the present time was employed as a legal secretary in the firm of Lowell and Hughes. And she was beautiful. He didn't need to refer to her medical chart to learn that.

After three days of observation, Dan could find no ethical reason to keep her in the hospital so she was released. She seemed pleased when he said he'd like to call her.

Dan called Liz at work the next day. "This is Dan Stewart, your kindly old doctor."

Liz laughed. She had a wonderful laugh, Dan thought. It was low and a little throaty. She didn't bray the way Susan did when she was amused.

"How are you feeling?" Dan asked. "Any head pain?"

"No," Liz answered. "But I feel like a perfect fool in the neck brace."

"Doesn't matter how you feel. Wear it."

Liz promised she would.

Dan said, "Could we meet for a drink when you leave the office?"

"Today?" Liz sounded doubtful.

"Of course today!"

"I don't want to sound like little Nell, but tongues have wagged. I know that you're married, Dan."

"I see," Dan said. "That's one of the things I wanted to talk with you about."

"I'm not a marriage counselor, you know," Liz said in

her clipped speech. "I'll meet you at Brinkley's at five-thirty." She hung up.

So far, so good, Dan thought. She knew he was married, but she was willing to meet him anyway. When he ran into Susan a little later, she mentioned something about dinner. "You'd better eat without me," Dan said. "I have to make a house call."

Susan gave him a funny look and walked away.

Dan made a point of getting to Brinkley's ten minutes ahead of Liz. He wanted to make sure of getting a booth. He sat facing the entrance. He hadn't seen her for thirty hours and he missed her. But when he saw her pause in the doorway looking for him, he was surprised at her beauty. She was wearing a well-tailored pin-stripe suit. Her glossy brown hair was pulled back into an up-do of some kind. What did he know about hair? Susan wore hers straight and hanging down to her shoulders.

Dan stood to catch Liz's eye. She saw him and her face lit up, making him feel wonderful. She was something! They shook hands, and Dan was surprised. Must be a British custom.

When the waiter appeared, Liz said, "Sherry."

"Sherry?" Dan was incredulous. "You Brits really drink sherry?"

Liz's eyes were dancing. "And what do you Yanks drink?"

Dan turned to the waiter. "I'll have a beer."

Dan looked into Liz's eyes. "I wanted to tell you I was married when I was examining your neck. But you might have thought me presumptuous."

"I might have." Liz laughed.

They looked at one another, smiling. Dan felt happy being with her. "It isn't much of a marriage."

"Then why did you? Get married, I mean?"

Dan couldn't take his eyes off her. The way she held

her head, the way her eyebrows arched . . . maybe he should answer her question. "I can't remember," he said.

"I can't stay long. I need to get home."

Dan reached for her hand. "But you can't leave now, not after we've just met."

Liz laughed again and drew her hand away. "I don't mean that I'm leaving America. I must go to my apartment where I live. My roommate expects me to cook dinner."

Dan relaxed. "You scared me. Don't ever do that again."

"I won't," she promised, and got up to leave.

Dan reached for her hand again and this time she didn't draw away. "When will you see me again?"

"I'll see you here tomorrow."

Dan watched her leave. When she was out of sight, it seemed that the lights had dimmed.

Dan and Liz met the following day and again the day after that. Dan wanted much more from Liz than conversation across a table. He wanted to make love to her, sleep with her, wake up with her.

Liz didn't flinch when Dan told her how he felt. "My roommate's going out of town for the weekend. Shall we spend that time together?"

Dan told Susan that old friends had invited him to go fishing in Minnesota. He'd be gone two nights.

"Yes?" she said.

Dan knew she didn't believe him, and he didn't care. The weekend with Liz was exciting and wonderful. She was his first love, his only love. They stayed in the apartment all weekend. When Sunday night came, Dan said, "Liz, I want to marry you. I'll get a divorce."

"Oh, Dan, I want us to be married. I'll marry you the minute you're free."

Dan planned to tell Susan that he wanted a divorce as soon as he saw her. The apartment was quiet when he unlocked the door at nine. He called, "Susan," and got no answer.

He found her in bed fast asleep. He thought she'd wake up and they could talk.

Susan opened one eye. "Did you have a good time?"

"Susan, I'd like to talk to you."

Susan flopped over and mumbled. "In the morning. Too . . . sleepy." Her breathing grew heavier.

Dan couldn't sleep in the same bed with Susan, not after this weekend. So he dug around in the closet for a blanket and spent an uncomfortable night on the sofa.

He woke up early and made coffee. He heard the shower running, and a little later Susan came into the kitchen, dressed to go to the hospital.

"I'm glad you made the coffee." Susan poured a cup and drank. "It's hot!"

"Susan, we must talk."

"Later, Dan, I've got to get to the hospital. It's the gall bladder. You know the one I mean." Susan hurried to the door, grabbing her coat on the way, and left.

Dan put the cups in the sink and went to take his shower. They'd talk for sure tonight.

Dan talked to Liz briefly in the afternoon. She seemed disappointed and a little hurt when he admitted he hadn't had a chance to talk to Susan. Before she hung up, Liz said she hoped they could talk tonight.

Dan met Susan in the first-floor corridor at six. He grabbed her arm. "Come on, we're going to eat out."

Dan took Susan to the neighborhood restaurant they liked. Over coffee, he said, "I don't know how to put this, Susan, but I want a divorce."

Susan didn't blink. "Why?"

"I've met a girl I want to marry."

"That's ridiculous," Susan said. "You're already married."

No one could talk to Susan. She was so bland, so self-assured. The only emotion she'd ever revealed to Dan was sexual satisfaction. "And you're being ridiculous," Dan countered. "That's like saying, you ate breakfast, so why do you want lunch?"

Susan nodded her head in agreement. "Prosaic, but a good point. Anyway I don't want a divorce."

"But we're not happy together. We aren't in love!"

Susan drank half of her coffee. "Speak for yourself. I'm happy with you. I'm in love." She smiled and slipped her left arm in her coat sleeve. "Shall we go?"

Even though Dan found another apartment and moved, Susan refused to talk about divorce. Her manner toward him, straight forward and friendly whenever they met, didn't change.

Liz and Dan spent their free time together, but Liz would not move into the apartment. As long as they weren't married, she told Dan, she wanted to keep some of her independence.

Ellen and David knew that Dan had left Susan. One night when Dan came to dinner, Ellen said, "Your father and I know that you and Susan have separated. Can we do anything to help?"

"Not unless you can talk Susan into divorcing me."

"Sorry," David said. "I had misgivings when I learned you two were getting married."

"Why didn't you stop me?"

"How?" David's question seemed to hang in the air.

"Has Paul been home lately?" David laughed. "I thought he liked Susan, at least at one time."

"We're expecting Paul home in two weeks," Ellen said. "He seems fairly serious about a young woman in

Springfield. He speaks of her often."

"I look forward to seeing him," Dan said without much conviction. "Thanks for dinner!" He kissed his mother and shook hands with David.

Ellen stood at the window, watching the glow from the tail lights until Dan's car was out of sight. "Don't you wish . . ." She didn't finish her question.

"Of course I do," David answered. "I'd do anything I could to help Dan be happy. Paul too!"

Dan had a short vacation coming, and it was due to start on Friday. He and Liz had made plans to fly to Denver and spend a long weekend in the mountains, but on Friday morning, he received a letter, sent by special delivery, from Liz. With shaking hands he tore open the envelope. It said simply, "This isn't working, is it? I'm going away. I don't know where, but I must get away from you. Forgive me and forget me."

Dan sat for a long time, staring into space. Liz was right. He couldn't allow her to waste her young years waiting for him. Dejected and disheartened, he canceled his vacation and worked through the weekend instead.

He continued to see Susan several times a day. Even if he wanted to, it would have been difficult to avoid her. As the days passed, they slipped into the habit of having lunch together, like the old days, before they married.

During one lunch, Susan said, "I got the Brandenberg!"

Dan was impressed. "The whole thing?"

"Every one of them. Come over and listen. It takes all night to play them."

They stared at one another and finally they began to laugh. "Don't mind if I do," Dan said. He knew what he was getting into. But what was the use! Liz had left to go

God-knows-where. Life with Susan was unexciting, but it was comfortable.

Chapter Fifteen
A Marriage Of Convenience

After Dan moved back to the apartment, life went on as it had before he'd met Liz. Susan seemed to have no interest in Liz and never mentioned her name. Dan never mentioned her either, but he thought about her when he wasn't working, wondering where she was. Had she gone back to London? Would he ever see her again?

In subtle ways Susan was trying to change, though several weeks went by before Dan noticed. She abandoned her comfortable flats for classic pumps with medium heels. She had her hair styled and remembered to wear lipstick.

They worked late at the hospital one night and on the way home, they stopped at a Chinese restaurant for take-out food. Susan had said she didn't feel like cooking. She didn't feel like eating either.

Dan looked at the untouched food on her plate. "Is something wrong?"

"Why do you ask? Do I look bad?"

"You look good." Dan studied her face and began to

smile. "You've done something to your hair!"

"No, I haven't." Susan's manner didn't change, but she blushed faintly.

"The black dress you wore to Bob and Sandy's the other night looked great on you. Have you lost weight?"

"A little maybe." No reason to tell Dan that she'd been dieting like a fiend. Susan looked into Dan's eyes. "Maybe I'm a little tired. I think I'll go to bed."

"Good!" Dan said. "I'll go with you."

Susan began talking about buying a house.

"That's crazy," Dan said. "We can't afford a house yet."

"It's not crazy. Mom and Dad want to give us the down payment."

"I still think it's a bad idea. We don't have time to live in a house." Dan could feel himself wavering. "All right," he said. "If you find something you like, I'll look at it."

That night, the telephone buzzer woke Dan at 1 A.M. "Dr. Stewart," he said softly when he picked up the phone, not wanting to wake up Susan.

"Dan?"

"Liz! Where are you?"

"I'm in New York, Dan. I think I should talk to you."

"Can you come here? Oh, no, don't do that," he said hurriedly. "Let's meet somewhere. Is Chicago all right for you?"

"Yes."

Her voice sounded faint to Dan. "Then go to Chicago and check in at the Drake. I'll be there late tomorrow afternoon."

"All right, Dan. I love you."

Dan replaced the phone on its cradle and glanced at Susan. She was sleeping on her side with her face turned away from him. He didn't think she'd heard him talking. He looked forward to tomorrow.

He lay down and closed his eyes, but he couldn't sleep for the rest of the night. Where had Liz been? Had she come back from England? Had something happened?

He decided to tell Susan the truth. Before she left for the hospital, Dan said, "I'm leaving for Chicago on a four o'clock flight."

"Oh? Will you be back tonight?"

"I'm not sure. Possibly." He could feel Susan's eyes studying him. "Liz Talbot called me last night. She wants to see me."

"Does she!" Susan put on her coat and picked up her bag. At the door she turned. "Then I'll see you when I see you." Her mouth twitched in a smile, and the door closed after her.

She was too cool, Dan thought. Or maybe she didn't care if he saw Liz again. He'd like to see Susan lose her temper at least once. She never raised her voice, never seemed happy or sad. Then he forgot about her and thought of Liz.

After checking with the desk clerk, Dan went directly to Liz's room. She was always more beautiful than he remembered. He took her in his arms. How wonderful to hold her! How could he have ever let her get away?

"Dan, wait," Liz said, "I can't breathe."

"Sorry." Dan loosened his hold and looked at her. "I'd forgotten your eyes were such a deep purple."

Liz drew away. "Dan, I wanted you to know. I'm pregnant. What should I do?"

For a moment he didn't understand what she was saying. Then he looked at her. Her breasts were fuller and she was even more lovely. Her arms were around him again, and he could feel her against him.

"Dan! You didn't answer my question. What do you

want me to do?"

"I want you to have our baby," he murmured into her soft brown hair.

Dan and Liz talked for most of the night, making plans. Dan would return to Oakdale and find an apartment. Liz would join him soon. Now Susan would surely agree to a divorce.

Dan got an early flight to Oakdale the next morning and was back on duty before noon. He saw Susan, and she agreed to meet him in the coffee shop for lunch.

Susan concentrated on her fruit salad plate. "Good trip?"

Dan took a deep breath. "Susan, I want a divorce."

Susan put down her fork. "I thought we'd been all through this."

"Things have changed. Liz is pregnant." He watched Susan's face for a reaction.

Susan dipped into her cottage cheese. "Congratulations."

"Is that all you can say?" She was treating him like a child, humoring him.

Susan waved at a technician who entered the room and attacked a slice of pineapple on her plate. "I could say you're a lucky man." She lifted the fork to her mouth. "Perhaps even luckier than you know."

"I'm leaving you, Susan. My things will be out of the apartment by the time you get home." He placed his dishes on a tray to take them to the disposal chute.

"If you decide to come home, the welcome mat will be out."

Dan looked at her, but she seemed to be paying no attention to him. He could think of nothing else to say.

Dan was happy being with Liz again. She was gentle, charming, loving, everything a wife should be. She gave him confidence and a sense of his own individuality.

With Susan, he always felt like an appendage, or a creature to be tamed.

Seeing Liz pregnant with his child made him proud and happy. Dan was sure of the future—nothing would go wrong. Susan would come to her senses and give him a divorce. Meanwhile Liz had never met his parents—he'd have to remedy that.

One day at lunchtime, Dan stopped in at the new apartment to suggest they drop by his parents' house tonight after dinner. Liz seemed hesitant.

"Dan, do you think we should? It might be awkward."

"They'll love you, Liz. And I think you'll like Mother and Dad."

Dan called his mother, and she sounded pleased. "That's wonderful, Dan. I've wanted to meet your Liz for a long time." Ellen paused. "By the way, Paul's here."

"Oh," Dan said, "it will be good to see my brother again." He put down the phone. "Too bad! If I'd known Paul was going to be there, I'd have kept you all to myself a little longer."

Liz squeezed his hand, but said nothing.

Ellen and David were in the reception hall, waiting for them. Dan could tell that they adored Liz on first sight. Ellen put her arm around Liz and took her into the living room. Paul got up as they entered.

"And this is our son Paul," Ellen said.

Paul smiled and extended his hand.

Paul was well over six feet tall and he towered over Liz. Dan watched them shake hands. It seemed to him that Paul held Liz's hand a bit too long. *Someday he's going to overdo his Abe Lincoln bit and trip over a split rail*, Dan told himself. Dan edged closer to Liz. "This is my brother, the legal eagle. How's the practice, Paul?"

"So-so," Paul said, never taking his eyes off Liz.

"I have apple pie in the oven," Ellen said brightly.

"May I help you, Mrs. Stewart?"

"I'd love it," Ellen said, taking Liz with her into the kitchen.

Then David received a phone call, and the brothers were left alone. After an awkward silence, Paul said, "She's a beautiful girl, Dan. What are you going to do about her?"

"Look for a good lawyer and divorce Susan. Can you help?"

"I'm not that kind of lawyer. I know a good man, but unfortunately, he practices in Indiana. You need someone local."

"I know," Dan mumbled.

"If there's anything I can do, you'll let me know, won't you?"

"Oh sure . . . sure. How are you liking Chicago?"

"It's all right," Paul said slowly. "But I'm not entirely happy there. I'm a small-town boy at heart. I'd kind of like to get back to Oakdale."

"That would be great," Dan said without conviction.

At 1 A.M. Dan got a call from Susan. He glanced at Liz. The phone had awakened her. "Yes, Susan," he said.

"We should talk."

"What's wrong?"

"Nothing. Everything's perfectly normal. Shall we meet at ten in the coffee shop?" It was a command, not a question.

"Sure. But could you give me an inkling . . ." She'd hung up! Why did she call at this hour? Had she decided on the divorce? That didn't seem likely. Dan kept waking and worrying, sleeping fitfully through the rest of the night.

Dan and Susan met promptly at ten. And Susan came straight to the point. "Congratulations, Dan.

Once again you're to be a father."

"Wait a minute! Run that by me again."

"You heard me," Susan said. "Our first child is due in May."

Dan put his head in his hands.

"Well," Susan said harshly, "this is hardly the reception a mother-to-be expects at the moment of truth."

"Susan, I don't know what to say."

"You could say, it never rains but if it pours. You could say . . ." Her voice faded.

Dan looked at her. Her thin lips were set and her eyes were swimming with tears. Susan was crying! He couldn't believe it. "Oh, Susie, I'm sorry. What a mess I've made of everything."

Susan was laughing and crying. "You really are a first-rate fool. And so am I!" Then she put her head on her arms and sobbed.

Dr. Shea paused on his way to a table. "Is something wrong?"

Michael Shea was the last person Dan wanted to see. "We're having a baby," he said.

"Congratulations!" Michael said and moved on.

Susan had composed herself and sat up. "And there's no need for you to insist on a divorce."

"I wouldn't think of it," Dan said, wondering what he could do. He'd have to tell Liz right away, and he dreaded the inevitable scene.

Dan told Liz that night. She took the news well, but in a way that frightened him. She was too quiet.

"I don't know what to do, Liz. I love our baby!"

"So do I," Liz said. "Everything will be all right. You mustn't worry so much." She started into the bedroom, pausing at the door. "You'll be moving out soon, won't you, Dan?"

"I hadn't thought about that," he said.

"I'll miss you," she told him wistfully. She went into the bedroom and closed the door behind her.

Dan moved out the next day. Susan was more determined than ever that they should buy a house. "We'll need the space," she said.

Dan told her he'd accept any decision she made. He called Liz every day and she always seemed glad to talk with him. Even so he sensed that she was slipping away from him—and he was powerless.

Paul called, inviting Dan to lunch at the country club.

"Thanks, Paul. But I'm a working stiff and don't go out to lunch."

"Then how about Saturday?" Paul asked. "I have something rather important to tell you. So try and make it."

Dan accepted. They decided to play nine holes of golf, depending on the weather.

They met at the first hole before ten. Paul took a few practice swings, loosening up to drive off. He hit the ball, watching it rise in the clear morning air, veer, and float toward a grove of trees. "I hope what I'm going to say won't upset you." He knelt to pick up his tee. "Liz and I are getting married tomorrow. We'd like you to be there."

Dan was thunderstruck. Two men were waiting to tee off and Dan waved them through before he said, "What are you talking about?"

"I can't allow that lovely girl to be humiliated. I asked her to marry me and she agreed."

"I . . . I guess that's very good of you," Dan said.

"Not at all." Paul gave him a pleading look. "I really love Liz. This way the baby will have my name . . ."

"Does Liz love you?"

"No, she's been very honest with me. I don't think

she loves me at all." He brightened. "But in time, maybe . . ."

Dan picked up his golf bag and slung it over his shoulders. "I don't like this, Paul. But there isn't a damn thing I can do about it. I should be grateful to you and I'm not."

"Don't you think you're being selfish?"

"Yes. Thanks for the game." Dan stumbled away, leaving Paul staring after him. *And to think the bastard invited me to the wedding,* he said to himself.

Liz and Paul had a simple wedding in the Little Chapel of the Oakdale Presbyterian Church. Ellen and David were the only guests. Liz suggested they postpone a honeymoon so they spent their wedding night at her apartment.

Paul had already made up his mind to find something to do in Oakdale so they decided to stay on in the apartment until Paul was settled. He hoped to buy a house. Liz didn't care whether they ever had a house or not.

Susan, meanwhile, found a house she liked very much. Dan agreed it was a good buy without even seeing it, but as it turned out, there was a lot to do before they could move in. Dan told Susan to take things easy.

In the ensuing weeks, Ellen tried to get Dan and Paul together. But Dan refused all invitations that included Liz and his brother.

One day Liz and Dan met in the corridor near her obstetrician's office. Dan grabbed her hand. "Liz! I've wanted to see you, thought about you so often."

Liz laughed nervously. "Excuse me, Dan. Late for my appointment! Ta!"

Dan watched her enter the waiting room and lower herself into a chair. Her beautiful body was heavy and distorted with his child. He turned to walk away and heard himself being paged. He was wanted in Maternity. That was odd, he thought.

He took the elevator to the fifth floor. David met him. "It's Susan. She's in labor."

"But this is only the fifth month!" Dan ran toward the delivery room and pushed open the door. Two residents were moving Susan to a gurney. "What's going on?" Dan asked.

"Sorry, Dan," Dr. Willets said, taking him aside. "Susan lost the baby."

Dan felt nothing. He turned and walked out of the room. He saw David and went to him. "There isn't going to be a baby, Dad."

David grimaced. "I was afraid for her. Poor Susan."

"Yeah, poor Susan," Dan said. He must see Susan, but he could wait awhile for that. He'd need to think of something to say that would make her feel better.

Susan recovered rapidly and was back on duty at the hospital within two weeks. She hid her disappointment and never referred to the baby. As far as Dan could see, Susan was her old calm, relaxed self. It must be wonderful to be like that, he thought. Then he remembered that day in the coffee shop when she'd cried.

Liz's baby girl was born early in March. Liz and Paul named her Betsy. Dan never went by the nursery to see Baby Stewart and he avoided Liz's room while she was in the hospital. He heard that the baby was beautiful. And certainly Paul was proud, as proud as he would have been had he been the father.

Through his mother Dan learned that Liz was going to work in the Wade Bookstore as soon as she was able to. They needed the money because Paul's job wasn't panning out very well. Dan was sorry about that, but knew he'd better mind his own business.

Chapter Sixteen

To The Future

Tom Hughes woke up to the sound of the rain hitting the window air conditioner. The sound was comforting. As he fumbled for a cigarette on the bedside table, he glanced at the clock. Not that he gave a damn what time it was. For members of Oakdale High's senior class, today was Commencement, but he chose not to attend. He wasn't graduating. That counselor, Mrs.-What's-Her-Name, had been right on the money. Not only did he fail to get into a college—he didn't even get out of high school.

Tom's father was furious and Tom was glad of it. He wondered if his mother knew of his disgrace. Maybe he should drop by and tell her . . . see how she'd react, or *if* she'd react!

He put on the clothes he'd worn yesterday and went out to his car. Maybe he should get something to eat. He had a kind of empty feeling in the pit of his stomach. He backed the car out of the driveway and headed toward Milton's Drive-In. Why was he going there? The crowd would be there, and he didn't want to see those kids. They'd all be talking about the dumb schools they were going to next fall. Dull . . . dull . . . dullsville. He turned the car around.

When Tom got to the street his mother lived on, he down shifted so he could case the area. Good! Her car was in the garage. He turned into the driveway, jumped out of the car, and raced to the front door. This was a real cloudburst! Lisa finally opened the door after he'd leaned on the bell.

"Goodness, Tom! You're soaked. You'd better get inside."

He went in and leaned against the closed front door, shivering.

"Come on into the kitchen and do your dripping on the linoleum." She gave him a sharp look. "What are you doing here in the middle of the day anyway? Don't you have school or something?"

"Not anymore. Today's Commencement!"

"Oh," she said. "That's different. It's about time for lunch. Will you have something with us?"

Tom wondered if she'd offer him pablum too! "No, thanks." He watched her open a can of tomato soup and scrape the thick, yucky-looking stuff into a saucepan. He'd had this sickish feeling for a week at least!

Tom leaned against the kitchen table thinking *she doesn't even know I should be graduating today! Talk about generation gap!* Turning away from the stove, she looked at him at last.

"Tom, what are those things you're wearing?"

He tried for an aggrieved tone. "What do you mean, Mom?"

"I'm talking about your trousers!"

"Oh! You mean my jeans?" Thank God! Something about him had finally registered with her. "What's wrong with these jeans?"

"They're filthy and ragged and awful! Why does your father let you out of the house dressed like this?"

"He doesn't pay much attention to what I wear."

"Well, I believe that!" She paused, listening. "Chuckie's awake! He's had a nice long nap this morning. Excuse me, Tom!" Lisa rushed out of the room.

He heard her run up the stairs. Then she was speaking softly. It sounded like baby talk. He yelled, "Gotta go, Mom!"

As he pulled the door closed behind him, he heard her say, "See you!"

Yeah, he'd see her! She didn't even know that he was a senior who didn't graduate. Some mother! At least his dad cared enough to give him hell. His grandmother had cried, and he was sorry about that. He'd like it if she could be proud of him.

After his father found out that Tom wasn't graduating he had talked to him seriously. He'd blamed himself. That was Bob's big ploy, thrashing his arms and moaning about being a poor father. Tom guessed he wasn't all that bad. But then he talked about summer school and how Tom could make up the two courses he flunked. No way!

But he had to do something. Tom knew he couldn't stay around Oakdale any longer. Maybe he'd go to Montana or New Mexico, hang out, get a job . . . a job doing what?

For several weeks, Tom had been thinking about joining the army. Maybe he'd be a big war hero! The army was somewhere to go, something to do. In Vietnam no one would care that he didn't have a high school diploma. And this time next week he'd be eighteen, old enough to get shot! Why not? He'd enlist today. Tom made a U-turn and drove to the county courthouse.

After he'd enlisted, Tom went home. He was feeling a

lot better, now that he'd taken some kind of positive action. And later on after he was on his way to wherever he was going, he'd call his dad. Right now a big scene might be hard to get through. He felt a little shaky. One thing for sure—he didn't want a lot of goodbyes.

Tom left Oakdale on the third of July with a group of inductees from down-state Illinois. They were flown to San Francisco. When he got some free time, Tom called his father from a phone booth.

Bob didn't say very much. Tom had the feeling his dad was crying. Could it be? He promised to send Bob his address, then later his APO number and hung up.

The news stunned Bob. Tom was a kid who'd get in the way during a war! He went back to the dinner table.

"Are you going to tell your parents?" Sandy asked.

"I'll have to. This will just about kill Mom. I think I'd better tell them in person."

Sandy got up from the table. "I'll go with you."

Nancy, who had heard them drive up, opened the door. "Something's wrong, isn't it?"

Bob nodded and Sandy said, "We have bad news. Tom's joined the army."

"How did you . . . well, where is Tom now?" Nancy reached out to Chris.

"He's out on the West Coast. He'll get some training and then he'll probably leave for Vietnam."

Nancy began to cry. Chris cleared his throat and said in a firm voice, "This experience could make a man of Tom."

"I'd hoped there was another way," Bob said.

"Does Lisa know?"

"I haven't told her, Mom. And I don't think I will," Bob said. He took Sandy's arm. "Guess we'll go now. We'll let you know if we hear from him."

After Bob and Sandy left, Nancy puttered around the living room, straightening pillows, folding newspapers. "It's times like these when I miss Claire so much." Her voice sounded a little shaky.

"She'd have plenty to say and that's a fact." Chris began to pace up and down. "The thing that gets me is, no one knew what was going on in Tom's mind. You'd think Bob would have known!" He paused by the window, staring out into the dark. "Remember when Tom was a little boy—how he loved that old tire swing in the backyard?"

"I remember," Nancy said, watching Chris. "You're terribly upset, aren't you, dear?"

Chris nodded. He couldn't trust himself to speak.

"Tom's going to be all right!" Nancy's voice was firm. "I just know it!"

"I'm glad you know that." Chris smiled at her and tried to feel better.

Bob had nothing to say on the drive home. Sandy broke the silence. "Do you mind if I call Lisa tomorrow?" When Bob didn't answer, she said, "She's Tom's mother and she has the right to know."

"Tell her if you like. If she were any kind of mother, she wouldn't need to be told."

Sandy called Lisa the next morning, saying, "If you're near the store any time soon, would you stop by?"

Lisa didn't sound pleasant. Her dislike for Sandy showed in her voice. "I don't plan to be in that area very soon. If you have something to tell me . . ." She waited.

"Have you heard from Tom?" Sandy asked.

"He stopped by a few days ago. I haven't seen him since. Why do you ask?"

"I thought you might like to know that Tom's in the army. He'll probably go to Vietnam. He enlisted."

Sandy wished she could see Lisa's face. Was she surprised, hurt, saddened?

"Vietnam!" Lisa exclaimed. "He never said a thing about it to me." She paused. "Tom's too young to be a soldier."

"He was eighteen last Thursday. It's hard to keep track, isn't it?" Sandy put down the phone without waiting for a reply.

One night, a little over a month after Tom left home, Sandy and Bob were just getting up from the dinner table. Bob was still in a deep depression, and Sandy, tired of trying to make conversation, was relieved when the telephone rang.

The call was from Ellen and it was brief. Sandy went in search of Bob and found him sitting alone in the dark library. She switched on a lamp and sat next to him. "Bob, I have to talk to you."

"I'm listening."

"Something has come up. Ellen's buying Wade's"

"Is she crazy? What will Ellen do with a bookstore?"

"She's going to give it to her daughter-in-law."

Bob sat up straighter in his chair. He was almost smiling. "Which one? Susan, I hope."

"Sorry." Sandy grinned. "It's the other one—Liz."

"Oh." Bob slumped back in his chair. "What are you going to do? Become a housewife?"

Sandy laughed nervously. "No, I'm going to New York. I'll invest the money from the store in a modeling agency. I'll be near Jimmy . . ." Her voice faded.

"You've been thinking about this for a long time, haven't you, Sandy?"

She shrugged. "Well, yes, I have. Then when Ellen was looking for a business that would interest Liz, I suggested it. Well, it's done," she said briskly.

"And where does that leave me?"

"Here, I suppose." Sandy sounded less sure of herself.

Bob sat forward.   "I've been expecting this for a long time. It hasn't been much of a marriage, has it?"

"No, Bob. And it's my fault. I . . ."

"No, it isn't," Bob said. "You never loved me and I knew that from the beginning."

"I'm so sorry." Sandy's voice was barely audible.

"Don't be."

"And I wasn't good with Tom."

"You were pretty good," Bob said, "As good as I was, and you did a much better job than Lisa did. But why talk about it?" Bob got up and walked the room. "You can have anything you want, Sandy. This house, the bank account, the shirt off my back."

Sandy shook her head. "No, Bob, I don't want anything. But I'd like you to find someone who would give you all the things I didn't."

"It's too late. Right now I don't want anything except word from Tom."

Sandy thought she'd better leave before she started to cry. "Good night, Bob." If he answered, she didn't hear him.

A week later, Sandy left Oakdale, and Bob put their big house on Country Club Lane on the market.

Nancy and Chris begged him to stay with them until he found a place that suited him. Bob thought it might be a good idea, temporarily. He'd have to think about his future and whether he would consider sharing it again. And he wanted, more than anything, to know what the future held for Tom.

For now, at least, all he could do was wait.

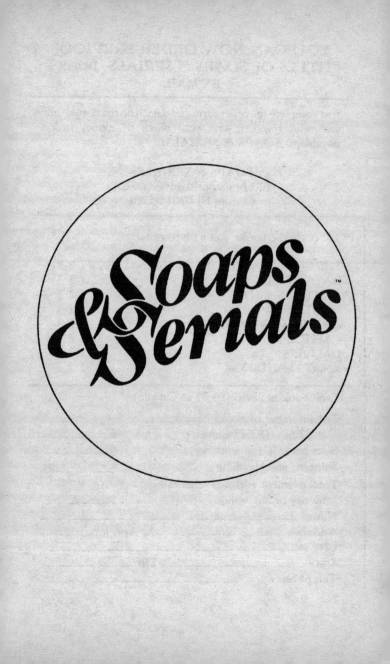

YOU CAN NOW ORDER PREVIOUS TITLES OF *SOAPS & SERIALS*™ BOOKS BY MAIL

Just complete the order form and detach on the dotted line and send together with your check or money order payable to **SOAPS & SERIALS:**

SOAPS & SERIALS™
120 Brighton Road, Box 5201
Clifton, NJ 07015-5201

- -

Please circle the books you wish to order:

THE YOUNG AND THE RESTLESS	BK #1 2 3
DAYS OF OUR LIVES	1 2 3
GUIDING LIGHT	1 2 3
ANOTHER WORLD	1 2 3
AS THE WORLD TURNS	1 2 3
CAPITOL™	1 2 3
DALLAS™	1 2 3
KNOTS LANDING™	1 2 3

Each book is $2.50 ($3.25 in Canada).

Total number of books circled _____
@ $2.50   ($3.25 Canada) $_____
Sales tax (CT residents only) $_____
Shipping and Handling $_____.95
Total payment enclosed (checks or
     money orders only) $_____

Name _____

Address _____ Apt. # _____

City _____

State _____ Zip _____

Telephone No. _____

ATWT3